THE MAGIC LEGACY

THE MAGIC LEGACY

THE WITCHES OF PRESSLER STREET™ BOOK ONE

MARTHA CARR

MICHAEL ANDERLE

LMBPN Publishing
PMB 196, 2540 South Maryland Pkwy
Las Vegas, NV 89109

First US edition, December 2019
Version 1.01, February 2020
eBook ISBN: 978-1-64202-614-6
Print ISBN: 978-1-64202-615-3

THE MAGIC LEGACY TEAM

Thanks to our Just In Time Readers

Nancy Weaver
Diane L. Smith
Kathleen Snowberger
Lori Hendricks
Sarah McKevitt
Rose Brooks
Claudia Pfennig
CJ Kilraoc
Billie Leigh Kellar

Special shout out to Grace Snokes, Lynne Stiegler, Judah Raine, Kelly O'Donnell and Stephen Campbell for their general badassery behind the scenes to keep everything running so smoothly.

CHAPTER ONE

"That protection necklace has to be here somewhere."
Laura Hadstrom tapped her cypress wood wand against the palm of her other hand. An old habit. She rose from the chair and lightly touched a line of old jewelry boxes, springing them open one at a time.

"Now you're just showing off." Emily stuck her tongue out at her oldest sister and tilted her head. "*We're* not looking for anything. You're the one who marched up the attic stairs. I came up here to help. I don't know why Nickie followed us. Don't you have a gig at ABGB tonight?"

Nickie folded her arms and smirked. "The band's off tonight, which you already know. And as the middle child, I'm pretty sure it's my birthright to be the voice of reason, here."

"Oh, yeah. Right." Emily rolled her eyes and muttered a spell, lifting a large rug covered in dust off of a broken armchair. "This isn't *our* stuff, is it?"

"A lot of it is… I think. We only cleansed the attic of old

spirits when we moved in." Laura rifled through the jewelry boxes pulling out a large brooch. "Lots of costume jewelry." There was an edge to her voice. "It has to be here."

"Look, we'll find it. We have magic on our side, times three."

"I bet we could find some really great stuff in here." Emily let the rug drop and coughed as the cloud of dust blew into her face.

"Focus, Emily." Nickie frowned at her little sister. "Take it seriously."

"Whoever lived here last left us all their junk and then we dumped generations of our family stuff on top of it all." Laura lifted her arms in frustration. "And I have no idea where it is!"

Emily waved a hand in front of her face, clearing her throat. "What are you looking for again?"

"The necklace that Aunt Julie gave me."

"She gave you jewelry?"

"Yeah."

Nickie went over to help her sister search the jewelry boxes. "The one with that weird little bird charm?"

Laura kept digging through the boxes as she nodded. "Yeah, that's the one."

"The question I have," said Emily, stepping carefully over what was either an old tent or part of a hot-air balloon—which was entirely possible in their family—"is why this is so important for you to find *today?*"

The oldest Hadstrom sister looked up at the far wall of the attic in the house she shared with her sisters, blinked a few times, and sighed. "It's special, okay?"

Emily snorted and shared a doubtful glance with

Nickie, who leaned toward their older sister and tried to bite back a smile. "You expect us to believe that you left something *special* up in the attic in all this... mess? You organize your junk drawer."

Laura turned around to lean back against the table. "Okay, fine. Dad *might* have mentioned something about Aunt Julie being at your graduation tonight, and I... well, I mean, she probably expects me to be wearing that necklace."

A sharp laugh burst from Emily's lips, and she clamped both hands over her mouth to keep it from going any further. "*I'm* the one graduating. Why would anyone care what *you're* wearing?"

"Em..." Nickie gave her the look she always gave when the youngest Hadstrom sister was about to take things too far.

Emily shrugged. "But seriously. I don't get—"

"She gave it to me when I made tenure, okay?" Laura leaned toward her sister with wide eyes. "She... made it for me with some kind of protection charm. *You're in a dangerous line of work.* She literally said that to me when she handed it to me."

Nickie chuckled. "Yes. We all know being a field archaeologist *and* a professor is just fraught with hidden danger everywhere you turn."

Emily giggled, and though Laura stood up with her back straight, she still managed a smile. "The protection charm was pretty weak." She tapped the wand against her hand. "I was wearing it the day I was looking for that amethyst artifact..."

"And still got stung by bees."

"So, it's not actually special."

"Which is why you put it up here in the attic."

"With all this junk."

Laura grinned. "I almost blew it into a million pieces that day. Tossing it in here was the compromise. But if Aunt Julie's going to be at Emily's graduation, I *know* she'll be looking for that necklace."

"Yeah, she does that," said Nickie.

"You remember when she freaked out on me for not wearing that ridiculous Christmas sweater?" Emily wiggled her fingers at a crumpled ball of newspaper and watched it come to life and skitter across the attic floor. "Her knitting skills are about the same as her magic skills. Mine smelled like actual reindeer. Do you think she did that on purpose?"

"We wore ours," Laura said. "Whatever you had against the sweater, you pretty much brought Aunt Julie's wrath down on yourself, if you ask me."

Nickie laughed.

"That's it?" Emily opened her arms wide. "Just leave Emily defenseless and laugh about it?" Her sisters immediately burst into laughter.

"You're the first one to pull out your wand and shoot off sparks at any sign of trouble."

"Okay, okay. I see how it is." The youngest Hadstrom sister reached into the pocket in her jeans and pulled out her wand. She lifted it with a quick flourish sending a silver spark into the air. "I know how to get things done." She waved the wand and the contents of the jewelry boxes rose in the air, sorting itself.

"Whoa, whoa." The smile disappeared from Laura's

face, and her eyes grew wide. Nickie chuckled again, but her smile faded a little too. "Em, be careful with your wand."

"Aren't I always? Come on, we're in the attic. No one can see us." Emily raised her arms and made a little show of lighting up different areas of the darkened attic. "What's the fun of being a witch if we can't use magic when we want?"

"I'm pretty sure none of us are in this for *fun*," Nickie muttered.

"And that's not the point." Laura stepped toward her youngest sister and pointed her wand at her. "Put the wand down, Em."

"Remember what Dad taught us. Never point your wand unless you're willing to use it. Oh, come on. You're acting like I'm some lunatic troll loose on 6th Street." She grinned at her sisters and let out another laugh. "Relax. I do this every time I can't find something special."

Laura waved her wand, overwriting her little sister's spell, letting the jewelry come back to rest in the boxes.

"Hey!"

"Which I'm guessing is all the time," said Laura, shaking her head. "I'll never find it in time."

Emily shot her sister a sideways glance, then looked around the attic and shouted, "*Reperio*, special necklace!"

The room went silent as the Hadstrom sisters waited for Emily's spell to reveal Laura's necklace. Nickie cleared her throat. "Wrong spell."

"Okay, right, I remember. *Reperio*, necklace!" Emily flicked her wand again, and a yellow light flared at its tip for just a second before every single item in the jewelry boxes came to life again and shot through the air toward the witch who'd summoned them.

The first one hit Emily square in the face. "What the—" The next two pummeled her in the neck, chest, and shoulders; chains and tiny, glittering charms and thicker pieces of costume jewelry jangled against each other and her before hitting the floor.

Nickie stepped away from the table just as Laura cried out in surprise. One of the wooden boxes had been latched shut, and when the necklace couldn't free itself, it took the whole box with it. The box thumped against the back of Laura's neck before sailing over her head and heading straight toward Emily. The youngest Hadstrom sister ducked just in time, and the jewelry box hit a tarp covering a carefully arranged pile of old clothes sitting on top of a trunk behind her.

"It's not just the spell, Em. It's how you deliver it that matters too." Laura rubbed the back of her neck with one hand and held up her wand with the other. "I'll take care of it."

"Oh." Nickie glanced at her older sister with an incredulous smile. "Laura Hadstrom's brandishing a wand just *to find a necklace?*"

"Em is right, we're in the attic." Laura shrugged. "We're kind of on a time crunch, right?"

"It's ten o'clock in the morning."

"Yeah, and I have a few things to do before we get to watch our baby sister walk across that stage for her degree."

Emily stepped out of the tangle of necklaces pooled at

her feet and shook her head. "Please, don't make it sound so exciting."

"It *is* exciting." Laura turned toward her youngest sister and raised her wand at the ready. "You're graduating college, and I—"

"*Reperio*, everything Aunt Julie made us!" The tip of Emily's wand flashed again, and every pile and stack of books and clothes and photo albums and things already forgotten jumped in every corner of the attic. The first item to whirl through the air toward the witch who'd called it was a pair of misshapen mittens. She caught them and laughed, slipping them onto her hands. "Look at that —" The two knitted mittens had plenty of holes and a few fingers way longer than any human—or witch—hands.

"Emily, come *on*." Laura jumped aside just in time to avoid an extra-large, horribly lumpy pillow with something resembling a cat crocheted on the front. "*Pessum*," she shouted at the felt hat, heavy with more lumps of felt roses than any hat should have to bear. The awkward accessory stopped mid-air on its way to Emily and dropped lifeless to the dusty floor.

"Whoa." Nickie lifted her foot as two green slippers with curled toes skittered across the floor. "Whose are those?"

Emily looked at the slippers and burst out laughing. "I've never seen those before in my life."

"Me, neither." Laura frowned at the green felt shoes. "You think Mom got rid of some of her magical mishaps in our stuff?"

"She would do that, yeah." Nickie nodded, her hands on her hips.

"Okay." Emily ducked under a stack of homemade greeting cards that were magically enhanced so the figures were constantly running across the front of the card, signing. She flicked the last stray cards aside with her wand. "So where is the necklace? Are you sure you banished it up here?"

The three Hadstrom sisters turned in a circle as the various items continued to float through the attic, dodging the last of them.

"Wait, do you hear that?" Nickie held up a hand. Something rattled like a pebble in a tin can, and Nickie stooped to lift the lid of a metal lockbox. The silver chain exploded from the open box, the tiny bird charm flashing in the dim overhead light. Nickie jerked back, and Laura pointed her wand at the necklace. "There!"

"Where?" Emily whirled around, jerking her wand arm out to the side in the process. The gesture sent Laura's necklace veering off course away from Emily and right toward the small, round window of frosted glass at the front of the attic. The glass burst with a little pop, leaving a hole just large enough for the not-so-special necklace from Aunt Julie to fly through, dropping from view.

"Oh…" Nickie let out a short gasp but Laura saw the corners of her mouth turn up.

Emily stared at the hole in the glass and slowly lowered her wand. "Whoops." She turned to Laura and raised her eyebrows. "At least you know exactly where it is now."

The oldest Hadstrom sister blinked slowly, glanced from the broken window to Emily and finally to Nickie. "Yep. Third bush from the front door. The one with the dent in the middle. This is becoming a habit with you."

Laura swirled her wand in a tight little circle, repairing the window before sliding her wand into her back pocket.

Both her sisters pressed their lips together in almost perfect mirror images of each other. "I'm going to go get that, and then I'm gonna head out to run a few errands. I'll see you guys tonight."

"Sounds good." Emily shot her two thumbs up, and Laura headed to the ladder that lowered from the attic into the upstairs hallway.

"Have fun with your errands," Nickie called out.

Laura didn't look at either one of them as she climbed down the ladder, shaking her head and muttering under her breath the whole time. Emily waited for the sound of her sister's footsteps to fade away. She looked at Nickie and grinned mischievously. "I found the necklace."

"Hey, that's not cool. She was really worried. Remember, we're supposed to have each other's back. Is Aunt Julie even coming tonight?"

"Okay, no. She called me last night and said she had to stay late at work or something. Before you say anything, Laura started it with her lecture downstairs about proper witch behavior out in public. I was sixteen the last time one of my spells went too far. It was just toilet paper in the trees."

"It kept coming to life and waving at people, letting out an awful moan."

"It was Halloween… Should be some kind of special dispensation for our kind at least one day of the year."

Nickie let out a frustrated sigh and ran a hand through her thick, long dark hair. A trait shared by all three of the Hadstrom sisters and passed down from their mother who looked the same except for a wide silver streak down the side.

"You have to tell her."

Emily only needed that gentle warning look from her older sister to know her time of having fun at Laura's expense was over. "Yeah, okay, got it." She pulled her phone from her back pocket and quickly typed out a text to Laura.

'Aunt Julie just told me she won't be able to make it to my graduation. Don't worry about the necklace.'

Laura's voice rose from the walkway in front of their house and could be heard clearly through the hole in the attic's frosted window. "Thank you, ancestors!" Nickie smiled and patted Emily on the shoulder. "Come on, play time's over. Next time, when I'm teaching you a new spell, pay attention to the wrist action."

Emily shook her head and followed her sister down the ladder. "It's like I have three mothers."

Laura Hadstrom made it across town as fast as she could. The errand couldn't wait till after her sister's graduation. "I've waited long enough already."

The thirteenth-century bronze dagger in her hand sent a sharp buzz through her fingertips and up her arm. "Oh —" Both her hands wrapped around the vibrating hilt so she wouldn't drop the thing. "You're really hummin' now," she said, looking up at the lone willow surrounded by green, shimmering water. "Okay, fifth trip here is the charm. Let's see what you can do."

Barton Creek was cold around her bare toes. She wiped her arm across her sweaty forehead and tightened her grip on the dagger. The smooth stones lining the creek were slimy with algae but still easy for her to maneuver. When she'd stepped far enough that the creek ran just above her ankles, she looked around at the landmarks and knew this was the place.

"Just one more step."

She turned to look downriver in case anyone happened to see a young woman in hiking shorts with a large dull knife in her hand stalking up the Greenbelt in the middle of downtown Austin. Thankfully, not very many people were willing to brave the muggy hike any farther than the first few swimming holes closest to the access road and the parking lot. But it wasn't Laura's bravery that brought her out here. She was on a dig in the middle of the city.

"I promised myself I wouldn't let this take me more than a month, didn't I?" She held the dagger out in front of her, using it as a channel to sense nearby magic.

Her mother liked to say that bravery drove people to do stupid things. Laura made decisions in the name of curiosity. "And stepping up to a good challenge," she muttered.

Consulting her mother's old books on local magical hotspots was a logical choice, but she'd found nothing about Barton Creek.

Behind her, a lock appeared in the tree, unseen, glowing with three quick pulses of sickly green light before disappearing again.

Laura moved from the empty creek bed and stepped downriver into shallow water. She faced the broad, shaded willow ahead, its roots beneath the murk of a slightly deeper pool. "Here goes."

The first step sent the dagger's tingle all the way past her forearm and up into her shoulder. The second step made her neck twitch. When she set her foot down on the algae-slickened stones a third time, a giant unseen hand pinched her entire arm from her fingers to her neck all at once.

"It's happening," she whispered. Her long brown hair fluttered in the blast of sudden wind and fell back around her shoulders.

She steeled herself for whatever the wards around the willow would do next. The dagger was her divining rod, and now that she'd felt the change, she *sensed* the wards.

After two more steps, the pressure and the buzzing tingle in her arm disappeared. Laura spun around in the water with only a gentle splash. "That's it? That was your whole circle of protection?" The sky was clear, the water flowed naturally around her, and it was still hot. Even the insects in the woods kept up their slow, pulsing hum. She lifted the cold, perfectly still weapon in her hand and shrugged. "Pretty easy. Now let's go figure out why I couldn't get this far without you."

Striding upriver, Laura headed straight for the massive willow. "Whoever put these wards here clearly went to a lot of trouble. And they obviously know a good deal about how this type of spell works. Well, so do I."

Five times she'd been redirected off course by the wards before she'd even realized how strange things got at this part of the creek. After all the expeditions, excavations, and surveys she'd attended, she'd learned to pick up on the signs and fit them together until they told her what she wanted to know.

"Hmm. Covert misdirection wards to keep people away? Someone is hiding something." The fact that there were also wards to confuse the memories of unsuspecting passersby—so they wouldn't *remember* there was something being hidden in the first place—meant there was *definitely* something worth finding. And Laura hadn't become University of Texas' youngest tenured archaeology professor by letting ancient magic turn her away from a discovery.

The minute her fingers brushed against the willow's thick, draping branches to pull them aside, the excitement of a new find petered out by something she couldn't explain. The tree and the artifact beneath it had both been here a lot longer than she thought.

Streams of sunlight poured through the willow's foliage. The tree growing up from a circular berm three times wider than the willow's trunk. On the berm, in the blackness of the enclosed shade, sat a large, round, white stone. It was the same size and relative shape of the tree stump Laura had sat on to take off her hiking boots, and it glowed where the slivered sunlight made it through to fall across its surface.

Laura let out a low whistle, then waded through the dark water toward the spot of raised land where just enough space allowed her to kneel on the damp, mossy soil beside the stone. Darker patches of moss and some kind of strangling vine covered most of the stone's surface. The top of the stone dipped into a nearly perfect round bowl, where none of the moss or vines grew. Peering into the depression, Laura frowned.

"Not limestone. Maybe not even from the Greenbelt. So…what is it?" She leaned forward to search between the stone and the willow's trunk yet only found more moss. A derisive snort escaped her. "I'm an archaeologist. Not a geologist. Do you know what it is?" She raised her eyebrows at the bronze dagger, then tipped it toward the stone. The tingling from when she'd approached the wards didn't return. "No. I guess you already did your job, huh?"

A series of lines ran around the lip of the stone bowl. There were too many vines to tell if they were simply weather lines or something purposely etched there centuries ago. "Like a message," she muttered. "Or a warn-ing?" She brought the tip of the dagger down upon the cool stone to scrape back the tangled vines.

Like a heavy iron lock clicking into place mixed with a struck gong, a huge, echoing knock filled the air, and it sounded like it came from right below her. The berm and the creek bed trembled. A loud, shushing noise rose from the stone like the intake of a breath, like waves crashing on the beach in one long, endless roar. The top of the willow swayed in a breeze she couldn't feel. Then, all the drooping branches lifted, some of their tips dripping with water. The willow was trying to become a bird, lifting its wings three hundred sixty degrees before taking flight.

Sunlight flooded over the berm and the white, vine-covered stone. The loud breath stopped. A hushed, word-less sigh of relief followed. *Like a Sprite commercial*, Laura thought, frowning at the floating willow branches.

The next second, a shimmering, opalescent light burst

from the bowl in the stone and shook the willow. It shook the berm, and Barton Creek, and Laura too. The dagger fell from her hand as whatever energy she'd unleashed blasted her and knocked her off the tiny island. Rolling thunder growled and echoed. Laura splashed into the creek, and a few of the willow branches snapped overhead.

The glowing energy coalesced above the stone and the berm, drawing more of itself together until it churned like storm clouds. It swelled beneath the dome of the willow and hissed like a snake the size of her house.

What the heck is *that?*

Laura scrambled backward through the water. Her hand slipped once off the slick stones of the creek before she reached into her pocket and pulled out her wand. "Whatever you're planning," she shouted, aiming her wand at the churning mass of hissing light, "don't even think about it!" She hardly heard her own voice over the ringing in her ears, though she definitely heard the low, rhythmic pounding growing faster and louder.

Are those...drums?

The energy drew itself up the undersides of the branches, then dove straight down to the water—and Laura. "*Nihil propius,*" she shouted, gritting her teeth as the massive energy source barreled at the bright-yellow, glowing orb at the tip of her wand. At the last second, the shimmering energy darted away and shot through the willow branches. The wildly fast pace of the drumming cut off, and everything fell silent.

Laura held her breath. All she heard was the ringing in her ears. *Either I'm still hearing the echo, or my ears are bleeding.* After a few moments, nothing happened, so she puffed out a huge breath and crawled, sopping wet, back up onto the berm.

"You're coming with me," she muttered, snatching up the bronze dagger and shaking her head at it. "There's a shelf with your name on it." She glanced at the stone bowl beside the tree and bit her lip. "That can't be good." Through the center of the round depression in the white stone—magically hidden for centuries until now—was a wide, jagged crack with burn marks around the edges. "Note to self," she said, eyeing the dagger. "Never excavate a magical artifact with another magical artifact. Whatever was in there, I think we just blew it up."

She stood and grimaced at her sopping shorts before slipping her wand back into her pocket and tucking her long dark hair behind her ear. It was impossible to tell if her hair was damp from her topple into the Greenbelt or just the wet, sticky heat that got into everything, no matter what. "Great. Now I have to go home and change." She checked her waterproof Timex Expedition. "Perfect. Just enough time to get cleaned up for my little sister's gradua-tion." Laura brushed the willow curtain aside and stepped into the suffocating light of the early-evening sun; Texas was one hell of a steam-cooker.

Everything looked the same—no massive crater in the Greenbelt, no pause in the chirping crickets or the droning katydids. A flight of grackles—messengers for the hidden magical world—took off in a rush from the trees on Laura's right, swooping low over the creek until they darted into woods on the opposite bank. And that was pretty much it.

"Well." She waded through the creek until she reached

the pebbly shore, leaving a trail of soaked stones behind her. "Guess we didn't find anything worth taking, huh?" This time when she sat on the tree stump, she left the dagger in her lap, glad it had stopped tingling.

"I have to admit"—she tugged on her socks and shoved one foot into a boot—"I thought we were gonna find some kind of treasure. Or a map. Maybe some witch's ancestral burial site. A Hadstrom relative, even." She sighed and shook her head, then finished tying her laces and stood. "But I have no idea what *that* was."

She glanced at her watch and nearly choked. "How did *that* happen? I just checked! Oh, *man*, I'm gonna be so late. I can just…" Laura stopped, cocked her head, and patted her pocket, feeling the familiar wand tucked there. Hesitating only a moment, she stormed across the pebbly beach toward the boulders and the Greenbelt Trail beyond while shaking her head. "Nope. Emily might pull out her wand for every little thing, but this girl here knows better."

CHAPTER TWO

Through the entire commencement ceremony, Emily just wanted to fast-forward to where she got to throw her hat into the air and start screaming. The other University of Texas graduates beside her shot annoyed glances at her rapidly bouncing knee. To calm down, Emily closely examined the cropped hair of the young man sitting in front of her and pulled her arm into the sleeve of her ridiculous graduation gown. Her fingers inched toward the long, narrow pocket she'd sewn into the side of her jeans two years ago until they settled around the smooth handle of her wand. "*Sile*," Emily muttered.

A girl with stage makeup sitting next to her shushed her, but at least the immobility charm had made Emily's knee stop bouncing. *If I need an excuse to use magic right now, I'll go ahead and call this a public service.* When her name was called, she had to quickly undo the spell and shove her arm back through the gown's sleeve before she could stand.

She walked up onto the stage and fought celebrating early and just chucking her graduation cap into the middle rows. Nickie and Chuck raised their hands over the sea of smiling spectators to wave at her, grinning like a couple of loonies. She grinned at Nickie and her boyfriend, then noticed their oldest sister, Laura, on the other side of Nickie, sitting beside their parents.

At least neither of them brought dates this time. Still weird to see them sitting next to each other.

Finally, the Master of Ceremonies congratulated them all, wished them well in their bright and glorious futures, thanked everyone for attending this momentous occasion, and invited them all to step outside for the fireworks celebration and "The Eyes of Texas". *Yada, yada, yada... time to scream.*

Emily jumped from her chair and threw her cap—she'd cast a spell on that stupid tassel before the ceremony so it wouldn't flop around in her face—and let it fly wherever the heck it wanted to go. A massive, triumphant bellow burst from her throat. "Freedom!" Because now she could forget about all the things *required* of her and do what she really wanted. And that was to be in her kitchen. *Chef Ansler's kitchen. Jeremy's right.*

Voices rose all around her in the Tower's Main Hall, which echoed with conversations and congratulations and the excited babble people had bottled up for hours under all this pomp and circumstance. Crowds filtered out of the Tower on the university campus. Feeling stifled, Emily bee lined for the exit. "I can get some air and wait for the fam outside."

It was a sauna outside, too, and almost dark. The Tower was lit up in orange 'in honor of the degree candidates', and people gathered in anticipation of the fireworks.

"Fireworks are not my thing," Emily muttered as she stood in front of a dogwood beside the path. A minute later, her boyfriend Jeremy found her and headed her way. "Okay. He said he wanted to talk after the ceremony. So, he's either going to express his undying love, or it's…the other thing." She wiped at her sweaty forehead with the sleeve of her gown, gave the sleeve an apologetic glance and smiled as he approached. "You officially did it," she said, wrapping her arms around his neck.

Jeremy hugged her with even more enthusiasm. "So did you," he said in her ear. He pulled away and grinned. "Whatever you think about it, it's still a big deal."

"So well done to both of us. You know, I think I've only seen you this excited about good food and comic books." Emily studied his bright-blue eyes, her heart pounding in her chest.

He glanced down at the sidewalk between them with a self-conscious smile, then removed his hands from her hips, as if he'd just realized he'd put them there. "And after college comes the rest of our lives, right?" His puppy-dog eyes took this conversation to a different level as he looked at her again and raised his eyebrows.

"Sure does." *This is still fifty-fifty…*

He took a deep breath and shrugged. "I took the opening in New Zealand. Bought my tickets last night."

She nodded and gave him a huge grin, not once looking away from those blue eyes. Now she knew for sure that she wouldn't be seeing them again for a long, long time. "Good. I'm so glad you took it."

"You are?"

"Absolutely. How could I be upset about you fulfilling

your dreams? I mean, you've been wanting to get into that program a long time. And you did." She reached out to touch his shoulder, though now it felt forced.

"I did." Jeremy chuckled and ran a hand through his hair. "I can't believe I did. But I'm going." He squinted at her. "You sure you don't wanna come with me?"

"Jeremy…we talked about this."

He closed his eyes. "Yeah, I know."

"I can't leave. Meadowlark Tavern is one of the biggest opportunities I have to get started. I paid my dues with school. Now I get to focus on learning everything a BA in Culinary Arts couldn't get me." Emily dipped her head and squeezed his shoulder to make him look at her again. "We knew this was coming."

"I know, Em. I know. It's just different now. It's happening."

"Yep. When do you leave?"

"End of July."

She stepped closer and slid her hand off his shoulder and down his arm. "We still have the summer."

Jeremy's brows flickered together. "I don't think that's a good idea. I need to be…focused when I get to the Institute. And that's gonna take me a little time anyway. You know. Now that we're…"

"Callin' it quits?" *It's like I'm helping him break up with me.*

Gently taking her hand off his shoulder, he lowered it and held it in both of his. "You're going to blow that entire kitchen away, Em. And when you have your restaurant, I want an invitation to the grand opening."

She laughed. "Deal."

"Okay. Good. You, uh…you still have a few things at my place."

"Don't worry about it." Emily shook her head and squeezed his hands. "Really. Those were gifts. Everything I left in your kitchen is for you. Take them with you."

Jeremy looked embarrassed, blinking and peering behind her into the shady trees. "Thanks," he said. With a tug on her hand, he pulled her close and wrapped his arms around her for probably the last time. He was trembling.

"All that training in New Zealand is really gonna add to what you're doing," she said, hugging him tight. "Who knows? Maybe I'll poach you as my Sous Chef."

He chuckled in her ear, then they pulled apart. Neither of them grabbed the other's hand again; he wiped his on his robe. "I don't think I'd be able to turn that down." They stared at each other.

If he kisses me goodbye right now, this would be the ultimate mixed-messages bag.

Jeremy cleared his throat. "Hey, can I—"

"*There* she is."

Emily glanced at her dad coming toward them down the walkway, his button-down shirt with repeated guitar print fluttering loosely around him in the small, hot breeze. "Great timing, Dad."

Jeremy shot her a questioning frown.

She shrugged. "That was sarcasm."

The rest of her family followed behind her father. Her mom wore a flowing dress, and she'd pulled her straight, dark hair into a high bun. All three of her daughters—Laura, Nickie, and Emily herself—had the same dark hair, yet only Emily had dark, wild curls that grew three sizes in the Texas humidity.

Laura walked a step behind their mom's left and was about as formal as she ever got in a cotton maroon skirt and Mary Janes. Behind her, Emily noticed Nickie's straight dark hair spilled across her bare shoulders, a paisley shawl wrapped around them. She wore two layered skirts and, knowing her, she could have arranged them like that for fun. Nickie's boyfriend, Chuck, walked beside her, holding her hand and beaming like Nickie was the Queen of England. *Nope. Just Austin's new Queen of Blues.*

"Both of you," Emily's mom said, glancing between Emily and Jeremy with a huge smile. "Congratulations."

"Thanks." They'd said it at the same time, and when Emily glanced up at him, he blushed.

"Good to see you guys," Jeremy told her family. "I should probably hunt down my parents though." He held Emily's gaze a few seconds. "Bye, Em."

"Bye."

He hurried off through the milling graduates and their own families, and Emily smiled at her parents. *Greg Hadstrom and Nancy Milton together in the same place. Not always the best combo.*

And mom does not *look happy.*

CHAPTER THREE

"Way to go, college grad," Chuck said and nudged Emily's shoulder with a fist.

Nickie laughed when her younger sister rolled her eyes. "Hey, for real," she said, "I'm proud of you."

"We are *so* proud of you." Their mother Nancy wrapped Emily in a huge hug and squeezed. Emily looked at her and widened her eyes in the way all of them did when their mom went just a little too heavy on the love.

"Where's your cap?" Laura asked.

Nancy pulled away from her daughter and looked her up and down.

Emily shrugged. "I threw it."

Nickie smirked. "I think I heard you pull a *Braveheart* in there too."

Chuck let go of her hand to throw both arms over his head, his hands tensed like claws, and called, "Freedom!" Nickie smacked his arm with the back of her hand and heard her dad chuckling. Her boyfriend faked a flinch and leaned toward Emily. "Way to be different."

"You're supposed to get it back," Laura cut in.

"Why?" Emily frowned. "I'm never gonna wear it again. And that tassel is the dumbest thing ever invented."

"It's symbolic."

"It's ridiculous."

Laura sighed. "You should try to find it. You might want it to look back on."

A giggle escaped Emily's lips. "What, you want me to frame it like yours?"

"Do I want—" A dramatic laugh escaped their sister as she tossed her head back. "No. You can do whatever you want with it. I'm just trying to be helpful. And I didn't frame mine!" Laura glanced at their parents, then folded her arms.

"It's okay if you did," Nickie added, trying to lessen the tension. "Nobody's allowed in your room anyway." *Because of all the wards she put around it...*

"Well, our baby's all grown up now," their dad said, stepping toward Emily to wrap his arm around her shoulder. "Now she's got the rest of her life ahead of her."

Emily huffed. "You gotta stop saying that, Dad."

"Well, it's true. And now that you're starting off on this new chapter we officially call adulthood..."

Emily rolled her eyes, glancing away.

"...your mom and I have a little something special for you. For all you girls. Right, Nancy?"

Their mom pursed her lips and took a deep breath.

"Mom?" Nickie asked. "What's wrong?"

"The Eyes of Texas" started playing beside the Tower.

"It's just not appropriate to discuss right now," Nancy replied, raising an eyebrow at her ex-husband.

Emily exchanged glances with her sisters. 'Not appropriate to discuss right now' was their mom's not-so-subtle code phrase for 'We need to have a conversation about magic.' And because Chuck was a human and had no idea that Nickie and her family were witches, that conversation wasn't going to happen with him around. Rules were rules.

"Let's go somewhere and sit down together," their mom said, forcing a smile. "Celebrate Emily's achievement."

"Hadstrom-family style," their dad added, wiggling his eyebrows. "I guess the surprise can wait."

"*Don't* call it a surprise, Greg."

He raised his hands in submission. "The final word has been spoken."

Chuck grabbed Emily's hand, and she smiled at him. "Anyone feel like hittin' up the Cat?" he asked.

"Yes," Emily said with a curt nod.

Laura just shrugged, and Nancy grinned. "Perfect."

"Then let's head out." Greg steered Emily down the sidewalk and bent to whisper something in her ear. She laughed and shook her head. Nancy and Laura followed them, Laura tossing her arm back toward the Tower as the first few fireworks shot into the air. Their mom just patted her on the back.

Chuck wrapped his arm around Nickie as they followed her family. "Laura's really upset about that cap," she said.

Her boyfriend bent his head toward her. "She's an academic professional at the school Emily just graduated from. I get why she might be a little peeved about her sister not showing a little more respect." He stared thoughtfully at nothing. "Then again, it's *Emily*. Kinda seems silly to take anything she does too serious. Unless it has something to do with food."

"Maybe." Nickie watched her older sister walking beside their mom. "I have a feeling Laura's got something else going on, though. The thing that makes her upset, and the thing she's actually thinking about, don't tend to be the same. My mom seems weirdly distracted, too."

"Nothing dinner at the Mean Eyed Cat can't fix, babe. I have to talk to them anyway. Figured you might wanna play there again soon."

She grinned. "That's a gig I will never turn down. You're not gonna make the whole thing about business tonight, though, right?"

He scrunched up his face in mock insult. "Do I ever?"

"Not as a general rule, no. I just wanna make sure we let today be about Em. She's worked hard for this."

Chuck puffed out a huge breath. "I know. School *and* that restaurant job? Does she ever sleep?"

"She did once. While making breakfast. Burned a souffle."

"Ouch. She raged after that, didn't she?"

"A little bit. I think she needs a break." Nickie rested her head against his shoulder. "I'm so down to play at the Cat again, though. Great vibe."

"And it's even better when you're on that stage." He pulled her close and pressed a loud, exaggerated kiss on the top of her head. "God, I love your shows. They're magical. You know that, right?"

Nicki wrapped her arm around his waist and leaned into him. *You have no idea.*

CHAPTER FOUR

The Mean Eyed Cat on West 5th Street was packed. *"Man,* I'm glad we got here when we did." Greg Hadstrom slapped both hands down onto the picnic table out back and grinned at the server headed toward them.

The girl carried an entire dinner for six on one tray. "Okay. This is pretty easy, y'all. Brisket all around..." She set their plates down and left the last one for Laura. "And chicken." The sides came down next, followed by the requisite packets of Wet Wipes. "Y'all need anything else?"

"Yeah." Emily caught their server's gaze and nodded. "Can you just tell the kitchen thanks for making everything last-minute for us?"

"I'll do that."

"Thank you so much."

Passing the sides around was as easy now as it always was for the Hadstrom family; they all ordered mac 'n cheese and coleslaw. Even Chuck.

"I still can't believe you got chicken." Emily leaned

toward Laura and peered onto her sister's plate. "Brisket is King here, and you're… defiling the throne."

Laura stared at her. "I like chicken."

"Yeah, obviously."

From the open door into the bar itself came the rising *twang* of a country-rock singer and the three-man band playing in front of the lit Staag Beer sign on the back wall. Nickie smiled and glanced at her boyfriend beside her. "That sound like Marlin Harris to you?"

Chuck chewed his mouthful and cocked his head. "Actually, yeah. I didn't know those guys were back in town."

"You know these guys?" her dad asked before chugging half his second pint of beer.

"Come on, Dad." Emily pointed her fork across the table at the middle sister. "Nickie knows every musician in Austin."

Nickie laughed. "That is so not true."

"But they all know *you*."

Chuck nudged his knee against Nickie's and smiled sideways at her. "Maybe not quite yet. But they will."

"Okay, guys." Nickie rolled her eyes and caught her mom's small, approving smile. "Don't let my career go to your heads."

"And why not?" Greg lifted his beer. "You and I are the only ones in the family getting paid to be on stage, front and center."

She shrugged and widened her eyes. "I mean, not technically. Shelly works onstage."

Beside her, Nancy gasped. "*Nickie.*"

Emily and Chuck both snorted and glanced at each other across the table.

"What?" Nickie tried not to laugh. "I stated a simple fact."

Her mom pressed her lips together and shook her head, though the corner of her mouth twitched anyway. "It's really not nice to gossip about your cousin."

"It's not gossip, Nancy." The girls' dad chuckled and leaned over the picnic table toward his ex-wife. "I bet you Shelly's sets are just about as long. And Nickie doesn't have to give private performances." Nickie slapped her hand over her mouth and stared at Emily, who threw her head back and cackled.

Laura looked back and forth across the table between her younger sisters. "I can't believe you guys are comparing a professional musician to a stripper."

Nickie tipped her beer bottle toward her older sister. "Hey, *we're* comparing on-stage careers." She glanced at Chuck and nudged him with her elbow. "Maybe we should make a bigger tip jar…"

"No," Emily added, "just take off your clothes."

Their dad's booming laughter drowned out the music and all the other boisterous conversations on the back patio just after 10 p.m. on a Saturday night.

Laura dropped her hands into her lap and rolled her eyes at Nancy. "Mom…"

"Laura, it *is* a little funny."

"Oh, my God."

"Okay, that's enough." Nancy glanced around the table with her signature 'cut it out or suffer my wrath' death stare. The laughter died down, and though everyone returned their attention to their food, there wasn't a shortage of smirking or shared glances. "I think what your dad was trying to say is that Nickie's the first *Hadstrom* woman to follow her passions for performing arts."

"Mom, I play blues."

Laura brought a forkful of chicken toward her mouth. "Is it still considered performing arts if she never went to college for it?"

Emily snorted. "What does that have to do with anything?"

"It's an honest question. I could walk around all day calling myself an archaeologist—"

"You do…"

"But it doesn't mean anything without my degree or my experience in the world."

"Archaeology and music are two wildly different things," Chuck said, forcing back a laugh. "Nickie doesn't need a degree to be a talented musician."

"I didn't need one either," Greg added before tipping up his pint glass again.

Nancy propped her elbow on the table and gestured toward her ex-husband. "Honestly, Greg, I'm surprised you're so willing to share the spotlight."

"No, I know she doesn't need a degree." Laura blinked and stared at the top of the picnic table. "We all know she's amazing at what she does. I'm *just* asking about the qualifications for something to be considered a *performing art*."

"I mean, she's *performing*…" Emily peeped at Nickie, stuck out her tongue, and nodded sideways at their sister.

"Yes, I know that—"

"Whoa, okay." Nickie lifted her hands in surrender.

Laura blinked again, blushing. Emily shoved more brisket into her mouth. Chuck rubbed his foot against Nickie's under the table. "I think what we *should* be talking about right now is the fact that our baby sister just graduated college. Right?"

Emily rolled her eyes. "Always the baby."

"Yeah, well, that's not ever gonna change," Laura muttered. "Unless Mom and Dad decide for some reason to—" She looked up from her plate with wide eyes to see almost everyone at the table staring at her. Only Nancy turned away, sipping her wine and pretending to be interested in the overhead lights strung across the back patio.

"What?"

"No, please keep going." Emily nodded and gestured at her sister. "I *really* wanna know what you were about to say."

Greg only chuckled and got down to business eating his dinner.

"I wasn't gonna say anything." Laura shook her head and went back to her chicken.

"Well, I've said it before," Nancy added, lifting her wineglass toward her youngest daughter, "and I'll say it again. I am so incredibly proud of you, Emily."

"We all are." Nickie raised her beer, and Chuck followed suit. "Tonight's totally about you."

Greg lifted an almost-empty glass. "To the baby."

The rest of them echoed the toast and clinked glasses all around. Even Laura joined in with her cup of ice water, smiling just a little.

· · ·

No one argued when Greg offered to take care of Emily's dinner and drinks. After they paid their tabs, Chuck wrapped his arm around Nickie's shoulders and squeezed her against him. "I should get home."

"Aw, come on, Chuck." Emily grinned at him.

"Yeah. I know." He dipped his head toward Nickie. "I have a meeting with Dave at eight in the morning."

"That's early."

"Well, the early worm gets eaten, and all that."

Nickie scrunched up her face. "What?"

"Oh, you've never heard that one before?" Before she could answer, he grabbed her face with both hands and kissed her.

"Ow, ow," Emily called.

"Cut it out," Laura whispered.

Chuck pulled away and winked. "I'll let you know how it goes. Love you."

"Love you too."

"And just… yeah. Bring it." He leaned over the table to offer Emily a fist bump, which she reciprocated. "Thanks for letting me tag along, everybody. Enjoy the rest of your night."

A round of, "Bye, Chuck," rose from the picnic table. Nickie turned to watch him walk through the crowded tables and back into the Mean Eyed Cat toward the front door, on his way to his car parked on the street.

"You sure got lucky with that Peabrain, Nickie."

She turned to look at her dad. "I know I did. Maybe don't call him that, though."

"Why not? It's a term of endearment."

Wrinkling her nose, Nickie shrugged and squinted at

him. "Yeah, but it just sounds weird when we're talking about Chuck. I mean, he still doesn't know."

"Well, that's his own path to follow," Nancy said. "It doesn't matter what he is, sweetheart, or whether or not he's woken up. He loves you."

Nickie glanced at her sisters and sighed. "Yeah. He's pretty awesome."

Nancy licked her lips. "I *will* say, though, now that he's gone, this might be the perfect time for the five of us to have that conversation your dad mentioned earlier."

"The surprise?" Emily perked up.

"See?" Greg turned toward his ex-wife in mock surprise. "I didn't say it this time."

Their mom closed her eyes, unable to laugh it off. "But it gives the impression we're talking about a present or a fun vacation or something."

"Well, the rings are gifts, aren't they?"

"Greg, please. It's much more than that."

"I *know*. But the legacy isn't a doomsday prophecy—"

"Whoa, whoa. Slow down." Nickie scooted away from her mom on the picnic bench so she had enough space to study both of them at the same time. "What legacy?"

"That's what we want to talk to you about." Nancy eyed each of her girls in turn and nodded.

"You mean like *our* legacy?" Emily asked.

"*Family* legacy." Greg reached across the table and patted his ex-wife's forearm. Their mom just pursed her lips at him and raised an eyebrow. "Been passed down through the Hadstrom family for generations. And now that all of you have come of age, which in this instance means you're no longer in school, it's time for your mom and I to pass that legacy on down the line."

Nickie glanced at her sisters. Emily stared back at her with wide, eager eyes over a huge grin.

Laura squinted, took a sip of water, then looked at their parents. "What kind of rings?"

CHAPTER FIVE

"Do you wanna take this one?" Nancy nodded across the table at Greg.

"I don't *have* to. You're part of this too, you know."

"By default. It's your bloodline. I just married into it."

Greg chuckled. "And then you got right back out again."

She ignored him and leaned over the table to grin at the girls. "Not before we raised three incredible witches."

"I'd really like to skip over this part." Emily waved her hand as if clearing away an awful smell. "Can we get to the whole family legacy thing?"

"Yep. I'm on it." Their dad scooted forward on the bench and laid both forearms on the picnic table. "This is what you girls were born into. Are you ready?"

"Dad…"

"Please just start talking, already."

"Yes. I am so ready."

"Okay. Let's start at the beginning. When this planetary ship took off from our ancestors' homeworld—"

"You mean Arenya V?" Emily asked.

"That one, yes. I can't tell you why the other races who left Arenya V decided to venture out into the cosmos, but the witches who stepped aboard came on as refugees."

"You mean they were fleeing." Laura bit down on her water straw.

"Exactly. Fleeing from another race that, as I understand it, spent a lot of time and effort persecuting witches and trying to wipe us out. This ship we call Earth was a sanctuary, so to speak. The Engineers took in the surviving witches with open arms when they recognized the danger. Our ancestors were among those who made it onboard. It took a while for anyone to realize a Gorafrex had slipped onto the ship. I mean, really, Earth's a big place to hide. But a few more witches turned up dead, and by the time the Engineers found the Gorafrex, I believe the ship had already gone quite off course."

"We know *that* story, Dad," Nickie reminded him with a nod.

"Right. I wasn't sure how much you remembered—"

"What, from every bedtime story 'til I started middle school?" Emily laughed. "It's kinda hard to forget."

Nancy glanced sideways at her ex-husband and smirked. "Keep going."

"Okay, ladies. There's a certain art to storytelling—"

"One might even call it a *performing art*." Emily snickered.

"Wow, I really left an impression on you, huh?" Laura nudged her youngest sister with her elbow.

"Can I continue?" The girls nodded at their dad, resorting to the silent promise of their childhoods by miming zipping up their lips at the same time. "Thank you.

Now, the Gorafrex couldn't be killed. Only... contained. Imprisoned. Our ancestors on this ship were the ruling family at the time."

"Dad, are you saying we're royalty?"

"Emily, stop interrupting," Laura chided.

Greg gave a noncommittal hum. "Think of it as more of a democratic society of witches. A cycle of different families ruling at different times. It just so happened to be ours, way back when. Those Hadstroms from long ago had a little help from the Engineers in creating a prison, if you will, for the stowaway Gorafrex. Our family has always had special gifts, right? Every witch family specializes in their own. The Hadstrom gift is, and has always been, in making the natural, the everyday, the mundane into something extraordinary.

"Take Nickie and me, for example. Our gifted magic lies in music, right?" He nodded at Nickie and winked. "We make people *feel* with our music more than they're used to feeling with anything else. And it's through music that our magic's the strongest."

Emily laughed. "You can compliment your other daughters any day now."

"Yes, Emily," Nancy said. "The Hadstrom gift applies to you and Laura too. You channel the strength of your magic through food, don't you? Your emotions. Your desires. Your passion. All of that ripples out into the world every time you create another culinary masterpiece."

"I don't know if I'd take it *that* far yet."

"Well, that's what it is, sweetheart. And Laura...well, Laura can spot a magical artifact from a mile away."

"How is that turning the mundane into the

extraordinary?" Laura stirred her straw around in what was left of her ice water.

Nickie laughed. "Remember that wand you found in the creek?"

"Oh, *yeah*." Emily bumped her shoulder against her older sisters'. "We all literally thought it was just a stick. Until you started casting spells with some long-dead wizard's *wand*."

Laura smirked. "Still took me two weeks to figure out how to access it. That thing was stuck at the bottom of the creek for...what did you guys say?"

"At least five hundred years, I think..." Greg looked across the table at Nancy, and they shared a nod. "Something like that."

"The point is that you *knew* what that wand could do." Nancy pointed at her oldest daughter. "Your dad and I had a few laughs over a soggy twig with a crack down the middle. But a ten-year-old who could find and *use* another witch's wand, before she'd even been taught how to make her own, is not something every mother gets to see."

"Yeah, okay." Laura rolled her eyes, but she was smiling.

"I've been wildly derailed again, here, ladies."

"Sorry, Dad."

"Do go on." Emily twirled her hand.

Greg cleared his throat. "Anyway, with this gift, our Hadstrom ancestors worked to shape that prison for the Gorafrex, using the gifts of our bloodline. And then, with that gift, they captured the one Gorafrex on Earth and trapped it inside that prison. It's still there to this day. And it's also the Hadstroms' duty to protect the prison. To be sure the Gorafrex never escapes. That's why our family's been right here in Austin since the beginning. We can't ever leave, because every generation has a job to do."

"The prison's in Austin?" Nickie asked, while Laura slurped down the last of her water through the straw.

Their mom nodded. "Yep. Right in the Greenbelt, actually."

Laura choked and coughed until her face turned red. Both her sisters peered at her.

"You okay?" Emily reached out to pat her sister's back.

"Yeah." Laura coughed and shook her head. "Yeah, sorry. I just thought Dad said there's a witch-killing creature in the Greenbelt."

"Kiddo, I *did* say that."

"Please don't call me that."

"Oh, come on. You used to love it."

"I know, Dad. And I'm not a kid anymore."

"But you'll always be my—"

"Greg." Their mom raised an eyebrow and spread her hands. "Boundaries."

"*Boundaries*? It's a nickname…" He looked to his other daughters for backup, but Nickie and Emily both shrugged.

"It was a very polite request," Nickie said.

Emily nodded. "You should probably just take one for the team."

"Wow. My own children…"

"Dad, are you gonna keep telling the story?"

He blinked. "It's all true."

"We know." Nickie gave him her most reassuring smile. "Which is why we want you to get to the end of it."

"You said something about rings." Laura pushed her

empty cup away from her and folded her hands on the table, her lips pressed together as she swallowed.

"I did say that, didn't I?" Greg glanced at Nancy. "You brought them, didn't you?"

"Of course I brought them." Their mom reached into her purse and pulled out a long black jewelry box. "I don't know why you had everyone send them to me—"

"Hey, we don't have to be married anymore for me to know that you are *still* the most organized person I've ever met. I wouldn't trust anyone else with something like this. And without you…" He wiggled his head and shrugged. "Well, the girls wouldn't be here without you, would they?"

"Ew. Dad…" Emily shook her head.

Nickie folded her arms. "Yeah, it was weird growing up. It's even weirder now."

Laura, meanwhile, stared at the long black box in their mom's hand, even when Nancy handed it over to their dad and shot him the 'watch it, mister' look.

"I wouldn't be your dad if I didn't keep things weird, would I?" Greg took the box and nodded at Nancy. "Thank you. Okay. This, my daughters, is the best part."

CHAPTER SIX

There were three rings in the black box—black, copper, and silver. They were thick bands and a better fit for a man's finger. "These," Greg said, spinning the box around the table so all three of his daughters could see, "are our family's rings. They were forged with the same magic that created the Gorafrex prison in the Green-belt. At the same time, I believe. As the story goes, because really, I never met these guys"—he chuckled—"the Hadstrom brothers who made these and began our family's legacy channeled the strength of their magic into the rings, so they could be passed down generations of Hadstrom witches until…well, I'm guessing forever, unless this rogue ship ever makes it out of orbit. Who knows?"

Emily tapped her finger on the table and squinted at their dad. "So… have those rings just been hanging out in that box, waiting for us?"

"Definitely not. I called Uncle Mark and Aunt Julie a few weeks ago and told them your mom and I decided to do this after your graduation."

"Wait." Nickie half-smiled. "Mark and Julie are part of this?"

"Well, yeah. They're my siblings, aren't they? Part of the Hadstrom line." Greg shrugged. "I guess, *technically*, your Aunt Julie's an Everett now. Doesn't make much of a difference, though. And since I'm the oldest and I have kids, the three of you are up next. So, they gave their rings to your mom and said good riddance to the whole thing."

"Greg. You're making it sound like an awful burden."

He chuckled again. "Because I'm *joking*, Nance."

"That black one's yours, isn't it?" Nickie nodded at the thick black band in the box, which Greg no longer wore on the ring finger of his right hand.

"Not anymore." Their dad pulled out the ring and handed it over to his middle daughter. "Now it's yours."

She laughed when she slipped it onto her right ring finger and the ring wobbled around it like a tiny hula hoop. "Okay. Guess I'm gonna have to make this a thumb ring."

"There you go." Greg grinned.

"That's what Julie did with hers, wasn't it?" Nancy shared a glance with her ex-husband, and, while she didn't exactly share his toothy grin, her proud smile was unmistakable.

"Yep. She did."

Laura leaned toward their dad sitting next to her and peered into the black box. "Nickie getting your ring makes sense, but Mark's a doctor, and Julie's a librarian. I'm not really seeing where the obvious choice is for my ring. Or Emily's." Emily stuck her elbow on the table and propped her chin in her hand, waiting for the scene to unfold.

"Well, which one feels right to you?" Nancy asked.

"Neither."

"Okay. Gimme the box." Emily reached across her sister to snatch up the open jewelry box in front of their dad. She plucked both rings from the padding, took one in each hand, and made a big show of sticking both fists behind her back. Looking up at the strung outdoor lights above them on the Mean Eyed Cat's back patio, she swapped the rings around and little, then stuck out both fists and nodded at Laura. "*Now* which one feels right?"

Laura sighed and tilted her head. "Come on, Em. We need to take this seriously."

"I *am* taking it seriously. You're just overthinking, as usual. I'm giving you the chance to turn that whirring brain of yours off a second so you stop thinking and *feel* it."

"I don't feel anything."

Greg started laughing, and Nancy shushed him.

Nickie nodded at her older sister. "You'll know, Laura. Just trust it."

Laura sighed, rolled her eyes, then closed them. Her hand hovered over one of Emily's fists, then the other.. She opened her eyes. "Can we just take these home? I've been working on this unveiling spell for artifacts—"

Emily burst into giggles. "We can take the rings home when we all have them on. Pick. One."

"I *can't* pick one." Laura's glared at her younger sister.

"Laura. Come on. You don't need your wand for *every* last bit of magic."

After a few more seconds of indecision, Laura closed her eyes and tried opening herself to *just feel it*. Emily glanced across the table at Nickie and winked. Then she closed her eyes too with a deep breath and focused on the energy of whichever ring just so happened to be in each of her fists. "Okay, fine. This one." Laura tapped her sister's fist, and Emily opened her hand to reveal the silver ring.

"Excellent choice. Very good vintage. Circa…when was it?" Emily glanced at their dad.

"Something-something B.C."

"Aged to perfection over millennia." She winked at Laura before her sister took the silver ring and stuck it on her thumb with a frown.

"Uncle Mark wore the silver one," Greg told her.

"And that means this one is mine." Emily revealed the copper-colored ring in her other hand. "This isn't just straight copper, is it?"

"Sure is. Pure copper. Pure silver. Pure obsidian." Greg nodded at Nickie and her ring that used to be his. "No, none of those things are particularly durable. But their original hardening charms have strengthened over time." He let out a quick laugh of surprise. "Aged to perfection isn't that far off the mark, Em."

"Huh." She turned the copper ring over in her hands and, just to be sure, rapped it a few times against the picnic table.

"Emily," Laura whispered in horror.

Nickie giggled. "What are you *doing*?"

"I'm testing the merchandise. And the word of the man who sold it to me."

"Dad's not *selling* these to us." Laura shook her head and blinked.

"Not for money, no." Greg shrugged. "The price is your

willingness to accept this legacy and continue protecting witches around the world from the Gorafrex in that prison."

Laura glanced at him and frowned. "Has it ever…gotten out before?"

"Not that I know of. Honestly, I haven't seen any activity there. If your grandpa ever saw something, he never told us. The thing might still be sleeping, for all I know. It's our job to be prepared."

"You've seen it? The prison?"

"From a distance." Greg smirked. "The wards make it pretty hard to get close. But I know where it is."

Laura swallowed. "Right."

"We should go down to the Greenbelt soon so I can show you girls where it is and how to interact with it. If the time ever comes you need to. Hopefully, it won't. How about tomorrow?"

"I'm in the kitchen all day tomorrow," Emily said. "Sorry."

"Monday night after I'm off work?"

"Uh, no go." Nickie shrugged. "I'm playing at Tina's laundromat."

Laura frowned at her. "Isn't a laundromat a little…"

"What?"

"Nothing. I just mean…hasn't your career grown out of laundromats just a little?"

Nickie laughed. "It totally has. But Tina's a friend, and I like being able to help her out on the off-chance anyone wants to see a show at her place. I've always got an opening there."

"I don't think anyone's ever turned you down for a gig." Emily spun her copper ring between her fingers.

"Please." Nickie shrugged. "I get turned down plenty. I promise."

"Right. Yeah, only by idiots."

"What about Tuesday?" Greg asked his daughters.

"After school." Laura nodded. "I could do that."

"Yeah, I just have a short shift for prep on Tuesday."

"Works for me." Nickie pulled both feet up onto the picnic bench, turned sideways, and leaned against the table.

"Perfect. Nance, you wanna come?"

Nancy shook her head. "Nope. I wanted to be a part of this tonight, but I think the rest falls on you. You're the Hadstrom."

Greg lifted an eyebrow.

"Why don't you bring that dental hygienist? Bethany... something-or-other."

"Beth Anne?" Greg scratched the back of his head and looked down at the table. "No. I mean, she's nice and everything. I just don't..."

"Oh, come on." Nancy leaned over the table in not-completely-genuine interest. "I bet she has incredibly clean teeth."

He chuckled. "Her teeth are fine, Nance. I'm just not into the cats."

Nickie and Emily exploded into laughter.

"How many cats?" Laura asked with a raised brow.

"A lot. Can't get away from 'em. It's just...*really* not my thing."

"Dad." Nickie stared at him with wide eyes, her mouth hanging open in amusement. "You're dating a cat lady?"

Laura laughed and quickly covered her mouth with both hands.

"Hey, we aren't *dating*. Just went on a few..." Greg glanced sideways at his ex. "Dates. The dates were fine. But the cats...hey, wait a minute." He shook his head and chuckled, his eyes crinkling into slits. "I'm not gonna bring a date with me to show you girls the magical prison our family built when this ship was so new it could still make it out of planetary orbit."

"Well, she's a witch, isn't she?" Nancy said.

"Yeah. She is. But that doesn't have anything to do with it, because Beth Anne and I aren't—" Greg shook his head. "This is a ridiculous conversation to have right now."

"Hey, Dad?"

Greg peered at Emily.

His youngest daughter grinned. "I think maybe you're getting a taste of your own weird medicine right now and you don't much care for it."

"*What?*" Greg turned to Nancy, looking baffled. "Since we're bringing it up, how are things with Mitchell?"

"Mitchell?" Laura stuck out her tongue.

"Sounds like a biker." Nickie lifted her hands and mimed twisting a motorcycle throttle. "*Mitch.*"

"*That* information is none of your business." Nancy closed her eyes and shook her head.

"What? You were just telling me all about the guy last week."

"Yes, *and*, right now, Greg, it's none of your business."

Emily made her own explosion sound effects. "Shot *down*."

"Such a double standard," Greg added.

"Well, I think we're both entitled to that now, aren't we?" Nancy blinked at him and gave him a tight, avoidant smile.

Her ex cleared his throat and turned to their daughters. "You gotta put on the ring, Em."

"Huh?"

"Put it on." He pointed to his own hand.

"Right now?"

"Yep."

With a confused laugh, Emily eyed their dad and gave everyone more than enough time to pay attention as she lowered the huge copper ring toward her extended thumb.

Nickie snorted. "Oh, jeez."

Emily slipped on the ring. "There. It's all—whoa." All three Hadstrom sisters gazed at their rings. A tingly warmth spread from their thumbs into their hands.

Nickie let out a wry laugh. "Did that go all the way up your arm too?"

Laura frowned at the silver ring on her thumb. "And down to my kneecaps."

"Nickie, what about you?"

The middle sister looked at them. "Somewhere in the middle, I think."

"That's like your entire body...wait. No. Nope. I don't even wanna know," Laura said, wrinkling her nose.

Emily gawped across the table. "Uh, where *did* you feel it?"

"Well." Nancy interrupted, bringing her hands down on the table. "I think that's enough said." She stood.

Laura looked up at her. "No, don't go yet…"

"Come on, Mom. At least stay 'til Dad's done tellin' us about our legacy. It's only…" Nickie checked her phone inside her purse. "Oh. It's already twelve-thirty."

Emily laughed. "Answer the *question*, Nickie."

Her sister ignored her.

"No, your mom's right." Greg stood. "It's late. And, really, I've told you guys everything you need to know right now. At least until Tuesday." He pointed at Nickie beside him, then swept his finger toward his other daughters. "Tuesday? Six-thirty?"

The Hadstrom sisters agreed and stood to hug their parents goodbye.

"Just remember," their dad said, "those rings chose you as much as you chose them. They'll make you stronger, pull your magic out in ways that'll surprise you. Trust me. This is from experience." He touched Emily's cheek, then wrapped his arm around Laura and then Nickie, pulling all three girls toward him for a squashed hug. "Most important," he added in a low voice, dipping his head like just another one of the girls swapping secrets. "The only way the rings, your magic, and the three of you can protect the Hadstrom family legacy is by using it together. Those things weren't made separately. They're tied to each other, just like all of you. Love you, girls."

"Love you too, Dad."

Laura ducked backward under Greg's arm to give their mom one last hug. Then Greg Hadstrom and Nancy Milton headed across the back patio of the Mean Eyed Cat.

He leaned toward her to say something with a devious smirk.

She jerked away and frowned at him. "Oh, don't even." Nancy sounded pissed, but then she laughed before they left the bar.

CHAPTER SEVEN

E mily shook her head. "Please tell me I'm not the only
one who thinks it's weird to see them like that."

"You're not the only one." Nickie patted her little sister
on the back and shrugged. "But what're ya gonna do?"

"It looked like they were flirting, though. Right? I mean,
didn't they do that *when* they were married?"

"Only when you were little." Nickie grabbed her purse
off the picnic bench.

"I'm only two years younger than you."

"I know. I think they're just good friends who had some
kids together and gave it a try. They liked the part with us.
Obviously. But they just didn't wanna be married
anymore."

Laura turned toward her sisters and cocked her head.
"Did they actually tell you that?"

"No." Nickie shrugged and ran a hand through her dark
hair. "That's just what I'm choosing to believe."

Laura shook her head. "There's no choosing to believe
something in a divorce, Nickie. They waited until Emily's

second year of undergrad to get away from each other. Which seems like a long time to pretend, if you ask me. They should stop pretending and just call it what it is already."

"What is it?" Emily asked.

"A divorce. The end. And they're still trying to hold onto something."

Nickie chuckled. "You think maybe that has to do with having three magical daughters tasked with protecting Earth's entire witch population? I mean, that seems like a good thing to hold onto. They're not gonna drop that just because their interactions are a little… weirder than normal."

"Well, now we have the rings." Laura fiddled with the silver ring on her left thumb. "And we have this responsibility now. So maybe they should finally call it quits and move on with their lives."

"You sound just a *little* angry." Emily pushed her neck forward and squinted at her oldest sister. "You sure there's not something else going on?"

"I'm not angry." Laura smoothed her hands down the sides of her cotton skirt and took a deep breath. "And no. There's not 'something else going on.'" She returned her attention to her silver ring.

"Okay." Emily met Nickie's gaze and mouthed, 'There's something else going on.'

Nickie nodded and started across the patio. "You guys ready to go?"

Laura trailed her finger along the curve of her ring. "I'm gonna find out everything about you."

Emily stopped beside her. "What was that?"

"What? Nothing. Yeah. I'm ready."

"Great. I left my car in the campus lot, so…"

Nickie turned around and spread her arms. "Yep. Mine's at Chuck's place."

"Okay. Looks like we're pilin' into mine." Laura followed Nickie through the back door into the bar.

"Shotgun!" Emily hurried to catch up.

When they pulled up in front of their two-story Victorian house on Pressler Street, it was almost one in the morning. Laura turned off her 2012 Ford Taurus as a neighbor across the street and a few houses down got out of an old El Camino and headed toward the front door of the blue bungalow.

"Hey." Emily pointed through the windshield. "We met her when we first moved in, right? What's her name?"

"I dunno. Margie… something." Laura removed her keys from the ignition and stuck them in her purse. "She always come home this late?"

In the backseat, Nickie shrugged. "I mean, I'm usually out a lot later than this. I don't really notice."

"Isn't she like a cop or something?"

"I think she's a detective."

"What's the difference?"

Laura opened her mouth for a pert reply, then puffed a sigh through her lips. "I honestly don't know."

"Huh. Maybe she's working long hours again." Emily squinted at the lights coming on in the bungalow.

"Yeah." Nickie unbuckled her seatbelt and opened the

back door. "A cop starting work at one in the morning. From home."

"I dunno. You think she's asleep yet?"

Laura opened her door. "No clue, we just walked in the door. And that's her business."

When both the car doors closed, Emily sat in the passenger seat and made a face at the dark sidewalk. Then she got out and followed her sisters up the cement stairs on the sloping hill toward the house. "Is it so wrong to wanna make friends with our neighbors?"

"No. But we have bigger things to think about right now." Laura fetched her house keys from her purse.

"Like what?"

"Like we just got magical rings from our very first ancestors on Earth and now have to keep a creature who wants to kill all witches from getting what it wants." Laura shoved the door open and stepped into the broad foyer leading to the stairs. The overhead lights clicked on, and she kicked off her Mary Janes. Laura started up the staircase.

"Hey, hold on."

The oldest Hadstrom sister turned around and raised her eyebrows at Nickie.

"What's going on?" Nickie squinted at her. "Seriously."

Laura sighed and deflated. "Nothing. Sorry. It's been a…weird day. Then Mom and Dad spring this whole legacy thing on us. I'm just…I need sleep."

Emily snorted. "I mean, he did say they had a surprise."

Laura shook her head. "Don't call it that."

Emily's mouth fell open, and Nickie pressed her lips together to keep from laughing.

Laura yawned. "I'll see you guys in the morning. And congrats, Em. You worked hard on your degree, and you deserve every bit of it."

"Not sure if that's really a compliment," Emily muttered. "But thanks."

"It is. Just exhausted. Goodnight."

"'Night."

Laura climbed the tall flight of stairs to the second floor and turned right on the landing. When they bought this house out of foreclosure almost two years ago—which made it affordable for the three of them to split—neither of her sisters had argued against her taking the master bedroom. Even though it only had an attached half-bath, and they had to share the one shower upstairs, Laura had seen the perfect bones in the master bedroom the day they came to check out the house; after that, she couldn't settle for any other room. It had all the space she needed for her museum—at least, for the size of it almost two years ago. She'd made her own additions since then.

The wards she'd placed around her bedroom door shimmered when she turned the knob and stepped inside. "Yes. It's still perfect." Her queen-sized bed in the four-poster frame sat in the corner just to the left of the door, the comforter, sheets, and pillowcases a soothing shade of tan but not too frilly. Her L-desk took up the far-right wall and that side of the back wall, ending just beside the door into her walk-in closet.

Laura went to the desk and scanned her neatly stacked piles of paperwork and forms, research materials, a few emails she'd printed. "She really should have gone back to find that cap. It would look nice in a frame." Laura's hung above her desk on the wall, arranged in a frame with her tassel and cord and her folded graduation robe. "Okay, mine's a doctorate, but a bachelor's cap for Em would look just as good." She glanced at all her other degrees, certifications, and licenses framed on the wall, then shook her head. "Emily's life. Emily's choice..."

"But *you*. Now we gotta figure out what to do with you, don't we?" Her fingers wrapped around the handle of the thirteenth-century bronze dagger she'd taken to the Greenbelt that afternoon. "Not very buzzy-tingly anymore, huh? Not that I'm complaining. You did your job. I just have no idea what that was." Dagger in hand, she went and opened the door to her walk-in closet.

A loud squeak came from the other side of the door as she opened it.

Laura stopped. "Egbert? Oh, boy. I thought we talked about this." She squatted and reached out to stroke the dark-brown quills tipped with purple that covered the *billynordle's* back. The creature wiggled in delight beneath her touch and nipped at her fingers with its short, round, bright-orange bill. The first time she'd seen one of these magical creatures, she'd called it a cross between a platypus and an echidna—with bright-blue legs and a green belly. "Actually, I *know* we talked about this."

Laura coaxed the billynordle onto her palm and stood, still gripping the dagger in her other hand. "I'm sorry I opened the door on you. And I know it's in your nature to be in the wrong place at the wrong time, my friend." Egbert ruffled his quills and blinked his large blue eyes. "But while I'm gone if you stayed in that cozy little bed I made for you , we wouldn't have this problem. Right?"

The creature swelled to its full size with a deep breath and chirped at her.

Laura chuckled. "Right. Let's get you somewhere safer."

The lights came on automatically as she moved through the reliquary in her closet, which was ten times the size it had been when the sisters bought the house. Laura stepped down a half flight of stairs into a room wider than her bedroom and extending beyond the house's physical boundaries.

"Okay. Here you go." She bent to lower the billynordle into the cardboard box lined with strips of one of her old shirts and a shredded ball of yarn. Egbert chirped. "I know. You put a lot of work into this thing too. So how 'bout you just stay there and enjoy it for a while, okay? Here." She opened the top drawer of a desk beside the foot of the stairs and grabbed some hamster yogurt treats to sprinkle in the creature's nest. "It's late, and you should be asleep. I have some work to do."

A bright-green blur streaked past her toward the billynordle's nest. A *skratchhok* climbed up over the edge of the box, its three eyes peering down into Egbert's nest.

"Hey." Laura bent down toward the creature, which could have been a chameleon with lime-green batwings if not for the third eye and tuft of white hair atop its head. "I *know* I fed everyone before Emily's graduation. You should all be asleep."

The skratchhok studied her for a few seconds, then opened its mouth quite wide and squawked.

"No. *Shh.* You're gonna wake up my sisters."

Another squawk echoed behind her, and Laura turned just in time to duck below the fluttering wings of two more creatures in various green shades. She laughed and had to shush herself.

"Okay, okay. Here." With another handful of yogurt treats, she drew the skratchhoks away from Egbert's nest and spread the treats out on the floor. The winged lizards scrabbled toward her on clawed feet, squeaking and bumping into each other to get to the late-night snack. "I mean it, though. After this, it's back to your perch. Do you really want to wake Inez up in the middle of the night and have to deal with *her* bad mood?" All three lizards froze, looked at her, and crouched low, making tiny, fragile squeaks.

"I didn't think so." Hiding her smile, Laura turned and walked to the right, where she'd charmed the bookshelf along the entire wall to expand as needed to accommodate all the artifacts, tomes, and trinkets she'd unearthed over the years. She passed her very first—the wand she'd pulled from Barton Creek seventeen years ago, before she'd come of age to make her own. That wand had started her collection. "And it's good to have you right here, front and center, to remind me."

Laura stopped a few feet down the floor-to-ceiling shelf where she kept her metal artifacts. She lifted the dagger and eyed it from dull tip to rounded handle. "We need to make room for you, don't we?"

She lowered the dagger toward the shelf, and the ring on her thumb began to pulse with a faint silver glow. With a low groan, all four shelves stretched themselves—and the entire length of the room—by another three feet.

Laura blinked at the ring. "I'd say that's going a little overboard, don't you think?"

The ring gave no reaction.

Sighing, Laura placed the bronze dagger in the empty space that was way larger than she intended and gave it a gentle pat. "You did your job better than I expected. And I think I need to go have a little chat with Carl about what we did today. I think I might have messed with our family legacy a little bit."

A huge yawn escaped her, and she turned from the bookshelf toward the long work desk in the center of her museum-in-a-closet. "We don't have anywhere to be tomorrow." She pried the silver ring from her thumb and put it on the desk. "Just one more hour. That's it. If I can't figure out what you do by then, I'm going to bed."

Setting her purse down on the desk, she pulled out her wand and held it at the ready. "Okay, Hadstrom ancestors. Let's see what you got."

CHAPTER EIGHT

Emily lay in her bed, staring up at the ceiling in the dark and turning the copper ring around and around on her thumb. An almost-silent hiss of air came from the foot of her bed. "Oh, come on, buddy. I'm trying to get to sleep, here." She sat up and eyed the chubby bulldog that had been in their family since the beginning of time, as far as she knew. "Speed, I'm serious. There's only one rule for you being allowed in here with me, and that's to keep the farts out of my room." Pointing to her bedroom door, she raised an eyebrow. "Do you need to go?"

Speed eyed her with droopy eyes and grunted, his jowls squashed on top of his front paws.

"Okay. Just remember, I'm trusting you to hold up your end of the deal. I didn't put a magical dog door there for myself, you know." Emily flopped down onto her back, but the stench worsened. "Jeez!. How does an immortal dog as cute as you end up smelling like a swamp beast on steroids?" She waved her hand in front of her face. The

63

copper ring on her thumb pulsed with a golden-brown light, and a gust of air exploded from her hand.

"Whoa." Swiping the blown hair off her forehead, she lifted her hand with the ring and stared at it. "Strengthening our magic, huh? Dad should've said it responds to every little thought. Gotta be careful with this thing." She took a deep breath, then paused. "Hey…the smell's gone."

Speed grunted at the foot of her bed.

"Don't push it, bud. I am *not* gonna follow you around like your own personal fan just to keep you from stinking up the place."

The glass of water on her bedside table started glowing, followed by a high-pitched ring like tiny wind chimes. Emily grinned. "Well, who's calling me now?" She sat up and shifted to the side of her single bed to peer over the rim of the glass.

Nickie's face rippled a little in the surface of the water, and she grinned at Emily with a little wave. "Can't sleep either, huh?" she whispered.

Emily shot Speed a warning glance. "I was *trying* to sleep. Speed's making that a little hard."

"He has his own dog bed by the couch, you know."

"I know. He just really likes being in here. Before I made him the dog door, he kept whining in the hall all night."

Nickie smirked. "It's either whining or farting, huh?"

"I guess. Why are we whispering?"

"I don't wanna wake Laura up."

Emily stifled a giggle. "I get that witches had magical FaceTime forever, but I really don't think Sister Soup was invented so you could call me *from the next room.*"

"It's more fun this way." Her sister winked. "I can't sleep at all. Up for a talk?"

"A talk without waking Laura?" Nickie nodded. "Okay. Clubhouse?"

"You're giving me crap for Sister Soup from my bedroom, but you're fine with popping into the Clubhouse?"

Emily shrugged and glanced at Speed. "Laura won't hear us. And Speed can't get in, so…"

"Okay. See you there." The water rippled in the glass, and Nickie's face disappeared.

Speed let out a pitiful whine.

"Sorry, bud. Even if we couldn't always count on you to gas-bomb the place, only three people are allowed in the Clubhouse. You're not one of them." Emily reached onto the bedside table and grabbed her car keys. She had two keychains on it; the first was a rubber chef's hat Chuck had given her as a gag when she got the job at Meadowlark Tavern. The second looked like a large silver coin, but its value wasn't monetary. On one side was a perfect thumbprint—Emily's thumbprint. They all had the exact same keyring. "Dunno how long Nickie wants to chat," she told the bulldog. "So, don't wait up for me."

Speed huffed.

Emily fingered the keyring, then slid her thumb over the coin until it fit into her thumbprint. A second later, her entire body tingled, and the Clubhouse magic did its thing, transporting her to the one place in the world no one but the Hadstrom sisters could enter.

She appeared in the center of the room, sitting in the exact same position as in her own bed. A paper lantern hanging from the ceiling filled the room with a purple glow, punctuated by tiny, floating orbs of light the sisters had conjured years ago. They never went out.

"Nickie?" Emily glanced around, then pushed herself to her feet and straightened out her pajama shorts. Her keys jingled in her hand.

With a little popping sound, Nickie appeared next to her and grinned. "Sorry. I had to put some clothes on first."

Emily laughed. "Okay…" She stepped across the room, which they'd decorated as kids in strands of colored lights, pictures ripped from magazines, and a few ridiculous origami pieces they'd made right after making their wands. "Man, I love this place."

"Always feels like being twelve again, doesn't it?"

"Well, I was ten when we made this…but yeah. It's kinda the only place that *hasn't* changed." Emily slumped onto the cherry-red futon and kicked up her feet.

Nickie fell into the brown rattan chair with the lime-green cushion and crossed her legs beneath her. "Mom and Dad were weird tonight, huh?"

"Yep. I thought they were just there for the graduation ceremony. I did *not* expect this whole 'let's reveal a secret we've kept from you your whole life' conversation. Plus this." Emily stuck her thumb in the air and eyed the copper ring on it. "I think these actually *work* magic."

Nickie leaned back against the round cushion and somehow made lounging in a bull-shaped chair look comfortable. "Dad said they'd make our magic stronger."

"Yeah. And I'm pretty sure they channel it, too. Like instead of a wand."

Looking at the black ring on her thumb, Nickie frowned. "For real?"

"I think so. I'm guessing yours hasn't done anything weird yet?"

"Not yet, no. Did yours?"

Emily shrugged. "I wouldn't call it super incredible or anything. Speed ripped one on my bed"—her sister snorted—"and I was trying to wave it out of my face. Little copper ring here flashed and *whoosh*. Aired out the whole room."

"That *does* sound like something you'd use your wand for."

"I know, right?"

Nickie raised an eyebrow and shook her head, trying not to laugh. "Which it really shouldn't be, by the way."

"Yeah, yeah. Laura's already given me enough speeches on that." Emily sighed and clasped her hands behind her head on the futon. With one bent knee on the cushion, she crossed the other leg over it and bounced her foot. "I mean, I get that we can't just use magic whenever we want, especially in front of humans. Not until their little peabrains wake up, at least. But, seriously, if nobody sees it and nobody's getting hurt, why does it matter? Like, what's the point of having magic if we can't use it to make our lives easier?"

"I don't think that's the point." Nickie studied the black ring on her thumb and shook her head. "Magic's meant to be a tool. Not a crutch."

"Whoa."

Nickie's head whipped toward her sister. "What?"

"You sound like Laura sounding like Mom."

"Whatever." Nickie smirked and brushed her hand

through the air like swatting away a fly. A black glow pulsed around her ring; the futon's front legs jerked into the air and sent the entire thing toppling backward with a thump. Emily let out a muffled shout of surprise.

"Oh, my god." Nickie stared at her ring.

The red cushions flopped around until Emily dragged herself out from between them. She rose onto her knees and grabbed the front panel of the futon's frame—now sticking up sideways in the air—to stare openmouthed at her sister. "*That's* what I was talking about."

Nickie gaped at her ring. "I wasn't trying to do that, I swear. I mean, if you were sitting next to me, I totally would've pushed you or something. For fun. But this thing just…"

"Yeah. Unintentionally channeled your magic." Emily pushed herself up and grunted as she dragged the heavy futon cushion toward her.

"My much stronger magic, apparently."

"Hey, I'm fine, by the way. Thanks for asking." Emily flashed Nickie a goofy, exaggerated grin and stepped over the red cushion to lift the back frame of the futon.

Nickie laughed and uncurled herself from the rattan chair to come help. "Sorry. You know I didn't mean to hurt you."

"Sure, sure."

They righted the futon frame and struggled to drag the heavy cushion back before slumping it where it belonged. Sighing at the same time, they flopped onto the futon beside each other and sat there a few seconds.

"I think you might be right," Nickie said, staring at her ring.

"Probably" The youngest Hadstrom sister smirked and cocked her head. "Right about what?"

Nickie laughed. "That we might be able to cast spells with the rings instead of our wands. Which would be pretty convenient."

"Yeah…but then I have a whole bunch of wand-length pockets in my pants for no reason."

"They'd be good for spoons, though, right? Or a spatula? 'Hey, line cook, where are the tongs?'"

Emily scoffed. "I'm *not* gonna walk around the kitchen with utensils sticking out of my wand pocket. And I'm not a line cook. The correct term in Chef Ansler's kitchen is *commis chef.*"

"Well, you should choose a better name than 'wand pocket', too." They both snorted. "Or use it for something completely different, if these rings are gonna replace our wands anyway."

"Hey, until we know for sure, I'm keeping the wand pocket. Wait." Emily glanced at the ring on her sister's hand and frowned. "That one was Dad's."

"Yeah…"

"I've never seen him do magic without his wand."

"You're right. I guess we should figure out how to put a lid on it. The last thing I need is to be rockin' out at a show and accidentally blast the audience over."

"Every musician's dream, though."

"Yeah, *metaphorically.*"

"I mean, this could be a huge break for you." Emily lifted her hands and spread them out like a news headline. "'Forget standing ovations. 'Blues musician knocks fans off their feet. Literally.'"

"Please. I could do that even without a family-legacy ring. If I played death metal instead, I could get away with it."

"Yeah, okay." Emily thumped her head back against the futon cushion, which really wasn't soft enough for that to feel good. "You think Laura's ring did anything weird yet?"

"Probably not. She probably passed out."

A laugh bubbled up from Emily's throat. "When it does...she's gonna lose it."

"Oh, my god." Nickie barked out a laugh. "She's gonna lock herself in her workshop and not come out til she's picked that thing apart."

Between exploding giggles, Emily caught her breath enough to say, "I don't...I don't think she *can*...with the...ring."

"Then she's never coming out!"

Emily mocked Laura's scowl she aimed at any item that didn't act the way she wanted it to; Nickie stabbed at an invisible workbench with an invisible wand. When their fit of laughter died down, one of the origami butterflies—complete with antennae and six legs—detached itself from its place on the Clubhouse wall and fluttered onto Emily's lap.

"Well, hello." She stroked the thing's gold-and-red wings, then it took off.

"Hey, I wanted to ask you about something else." Nickie ran a hand through her hair, tossing the ends of it over her shoulder, and leaned sideways against the back of the cushion, facing Emily.

"Sure. I'll make you breakfast tomorrow. You don't have to beg or anything." Emily rolled her eyes.

"Okay." Nickie chuckled. "But that's not it."

"Threw myself under the bus, didn't I?" Emily wrinkled her nose.

"I just wanted to ask if you're okay."

"Uh yeah. Why wouldn't I be?"

Nickie tipped her head side to side a few times. "Well, I saw you and Jeremy talking after the ceremony. It looked kinda serious."

"Hmm." Emily clenched her eyes shut and grimaced. "I think it was a lot more serious for him than it was for me. I'm pretty sure we broke up."

"What?"

"Yeah…"

"Why? What happened?"

Emily shrugged. "He got accepted into a culinary institute in New Zealand. He's leaving at the end of the summer for the fall semester."

Nickie blinked. "And he doesn't want you to go with him?"

"Oh, he definitely wants me to. I'm the one who doesn't wanna drop my whole life and move to a different country." Emily scratched her head, then tossed the hair out of her face. "I *know* that working at Meadowlark Tavern is gonna get me exactly where I wanna be. In my own kitchen. My own place. And until I've learned everything I can there, I can't start over again somewhere else. Not even for Jeremy."

"Yeah, that doesn't surprise me. Still, you guys were together for a while, right?"

"Almost two years."

"And you're not…upset? Even a little?"

Emily rolled her eyes. "I mean, yeah. A little. I definitely care about him, but it's not like we had anything close to something like you and Chuck. That's without looking at the whole career part of it."

"What do you mean?"

"Like, Chuck's your manager. But it's not because he just gave up trying to be a musician. And he's not trying to compete with you in a weird way."

Nickie snorted. "Yeah, his only musical talent is finding talented musicians."

"Right. Jeremy and I have the same passion, right? Food. I want to have my own place. I don't think he could handle all the extra stuff that comes with that. I mean, he'll probably end up being a head chef somewhere in a fantastic restaurant, creating whatever he wants. But there was just always this weird kind of competition going on. Mostly from him. I think he was hoping I'd change my mind."

"So, he broke up with you?"

Emily winced and laughed. "Not really. I said we still had the summer to spend time together before he leaves, but he basically shot that down. I guess…'cause it would be too hard for him? Kinda felt like *I* had to break up with him just to let him off the hook."

"Bummer."

"It's fine. I'm fine." Emily peered at her older sister and smiled. "All good."

"Okay. Well, if you wanna talk at all, I'm here."

"Yeah. I'll just Sister-Soup you in the middle of the night and drag you here. Way too much work to walk across the hall."

"Ha ha." Nickie stuck her tongue out, and Emily was attacked by a massive yawn.

"I think I'm ready to pass out too."

"Yeah, it's late." Both sisters grabbed their coin keyrings —Nickie hadn't put any keys on hers—and held them at the ready. "I'm gonna hold you to that breakfast thing, though."

Emily rolled her eyes. "Fine. But just waffles, so don't expect anything fancy."

"Em, your waffles are never 'just waffles.'" Nickie grinned, then slid her thumb over the thumbprint on her keyring and disappeared.

"Great." Emily snorted. "That's like saying I should just open my own magical Waffle House and call it good." She shook her head, then thumbed her keyring and returned to her bed in her own room.

Out cold at the foot of her bed, Speed snored through his squashed nose.

At least it doesn't smell like something died in here. Emily squirmed under the covers, dropped her head onto the pillow, and fell asleep in less than a minute.

CHAPTER NINE

The minute Laura woke up the next morning, she slammed her hand down on her bedside table and grabbed her phone. "Seven-thirty? Jeez, did I stay up later than I thought?" She rubbed her cheeks and sat up in bed. Glancing at the silver ring on her right hand, she frowned. "You're a tough one to crack, aren't you? Don't worry. We'll get there."

She tossed the covers off and swung her feet onto the floor. After tying her hair into a loose ponytail, she grabbed her zip-up hoodie from the dresser beside her bed and pulled it on. "Just until I can get some coffee to warm me up."

The smell of Emily's waffles filled the upstairs hallway and made her mouth water. "How are they awake before me?" She went downstairs and turned left past the sunroom and into the kitchen, stepping into her sisters' conversation.

"Really, Em, it's okay. These are great."

"No. It's *not* okay." Emily swiped her hand across the

spice rack against the full length of the long kitchen counter beside the stove. All her bottles of spices, herbs, powders, and salts moved down the line away from her on a magical conveyor belt; the new bottles closest to her popped into existence at the front, and those at the end of the line disappeared into the far kitchen wall when she sent them that way. "It's not okay, because I didn't even put mint *in* the batter."

Nickie turned in her chair and raised her eyebrows. "I said it was refreshing, Emily."

"Refreshing means minty. Cooling. Airy. And I tasted it myself, Nickie. It's not *minty*." Emily whirled around from the counter, her never-ending spice rack clicking at high speeds as the bottles appeared on one end and disappeared on the other. She caught sight of Laura standing in the entryway and slumped her shoulders in defeat. "I don't know what I did."

"I'm sure it's not as bad as you think." Laura headed toward the table, eyeing the plate of waffles in front of Nickie.

Nickie sat back in her chair and gestured for her big sister to take a stab at it. Laura grabbed the fork and took a bite. "Emily, I don't know what you're talking about," she said around the mouthful. "This is delicious."

"Yeah, I know, but that's not the problem."

Laura blinked at her. "What's the problem?"

"The *problem* is I put cinnamon and cardamom and a little bit of vanilla in the batter. Plus the new—oh. Crap." She spun around and reached out for the spice rack, jerking it toward her this time so the line of bottles flew in the opposite direction.

Laura took another bite, then handed the fork to Nickie and headed for the hot pot of coffee by the fridge. She stirred in two teaspoons of sugar as Emily still groaned in frustration. "So what happened?" Laura put the spoon down on the serving tray and lifted the mug to her lips.

"I grabbed the wrong bottle," Emily muttered. She slammed her hands on the counter and hunched her shoulders.

"Was it mint?" Nickie jammed another bite of waffle into her mouth.

"No. I meant to grab the honey powder. The hyssop's next to it."

"And hyssop tastes like mint?" Laura blew across the top of her coffee as she sat at the round table next to Nickie.

"It does to me." Emily shook her head, turned around, and leaned back against the counter. "Sorry. You don't have to keep eating that just to make me feel better."

Nickie snorted. "I'm not gonna eat something I don't like." More waffle went right into her mouth. "I think you're onto something with the hyssop waffles." She shrugged.

"Yeah, well, now I'm gonna make them the right way. Laura, you want *real* waffles?"

"Sure."

Emily spun around and started whipping up new batter, paying more attention to which bottles she snatched from her rack.

"So." Nickie pushed her empty plate away and ran a hand through her hair. "What do you think about your ring?"

Laura eyed her over the rim of her mug and took a long, slow sip of coffee. "I dunno. What do you think about yours?"

"She's trying to ask you if your ring's done any magic yet," Emily said, tossing a hand over her shoulder without turning from the counter.

"That happened to you guys too?" Laura set her coffee down and watched her sisters' reactions. They nodded. "Yeah. Mine activated my...uh, just an accommodation charm I set up in my closet." Nickie raised an eyebrow. "I just wanted to make a *little* extra space, but I didn't touch anything or cast a single spell. The ring glowed a little, and I got, well, a lot more room than I expected."

"Huh." Nickie smirked. "Em, I think I might have the most powerful ring."

Emily threw her head back to groan up at the ceiling. "Of course you do! Jeez, Nick, this isn't 'one ring to rule them all.' It's not a flipping competition."

The middle Hadstrom sister chuckled and sat back in her chair. But she widened her eyes at Laura and pointed her thumb toward Emily, who'd clearly woken up on the wrong side of the bed.

"Okay, I'll bite. What do you mean by 'most powerful'?" Laura asked.

"Well, yours activated a charm. Angry Chef over here had, what? A blast of air come out of hers, I guess." On cue, Speed waddled into the kitchen, his collar tags jingling as he puffed and snorted their way. "To clear away this guy's blast of air."

"Gross." Laura leaned in her chair and scratched the bulldog behind the ears. He slumped to his belly on the floor, back legs splayed out like a leaping frog. "What about your ring?"

Nickie waved her hand. "Mine knocked over the futon."

"Futon…" Laura frowned. "In the Clubhouse?"

Both sisters said, "Yep," at the same time.

"When were you guys in the Clubhouse?"

"Last night. We couldn't sleep—"

"*You* couldn't sleep." Emily pointed a batter-smeared spatula at the kitchen table without turning around.

"Neither could you with Mr. McStinky here as a foot-warmer." Speed licked his jowls and grunted. "We didn't wanna be loud and wake you up."

Laura cupped the coffee mug in her hands, letting it warm her up. "You wouldn't have. I was trying to figure out why my ring was using magic on its own." Both her sisters burst out laughing, and Laura glanced between them with a clueless smile. "Why is that funny?"

"We called it," Emily said, opening the waffle-maker next to the stove. "We just thought it would take a little longer. You were pretty convincing with your whole 'long day, I just need sleep' spiel."

"I *was* actually tired, okay? I was just putting a few things away before bed, then the ring acted up. I couldn't go to sleep without trying to figure it out first."

"Did you?" Nickie folded her arms.

"No. Nothing. As far as I can tell, unless I'm wearing the thing, it's just a super-hard piece of jewelry."

The new batch of waffle batter sizzled on the griddle as Emily poured it into each of the four round molds. "That's a good thing, right? Means the rings only work if *we're* wearing them."

Nickie chuckled. "Why would anyone else be wearing our family rings?"

"I dunno. People steal all kinds of things for no apparent reason. Creatures too." With the spatula, Emily scraped the rest of the batter out of the bowl and evenly onto the molds. "Remember that striped neon scarf Jeremy gave me for Christmas last year?"

"Yeah, that thing was awful." Nickie and Laura shared a knowing glance.

"I know. It was perfect." Emily closed the waffle-maker and turned around. "That got stolen. I'm pretty sure a *gorlek* took it. Haven't seen one of those since…middle school, probably."

Laura almost sprayed coffee all over the table. "Why do you think that?"

Emily spread her arms. "What else leaves feathers *and* slime? The thing left a trail all over my dresser."

"Huh." *That was definitely Inez. Now I'm gonna have to find that scarf!* Laura took a slow sip. "Maybe it's a good idea to keep the rings on all the time, then, right? I never saw Dad without his."

"Yeah, that was weird. I didn't even notice he wasn't wearing it 'til he opened that box last night." Nickie shrugged. "I can keep it on all the time. Sure."

"I can try," Emily said. "Chef makes Evaline take off her wedding ring on the line. But the rock on that thing's almost as big as her hand. As long as this one doesn't mess with my work, then yeah. I can keep it on."

"Cool." Laura sipped her coffee and watched her youngest sister pry her perfect, fancy waffles out of the waffle-maker and onto two plates.

"Want any more?" Emily asked Nickie.

"I'm stuffed."

Emily shrugged and brought both plates to the table. "Looks like you get the *real* batch." She slid one plate across the table toward Laura. "I swear, if these don't taste the way they're supposed to I'm gonna break something."

"Whoa." Nickie and Laura shared another glance. "You okay?"

"Yep." Emily slathered butter over her waffles before passing the butter dish to Laura. She drizzled syrup on them, thumped the container onto the table, and froze. "Maybe." Emily sighed. "Got a text this morning that I'm moving to a different station today. And of course no one's gonna tell me if I'm moving 'cause I qualify for *legumier* expertise or 'cause I screwed something up and Ben just wants me out of his space." Pressing her lips together, she attacked the first waffle with her fork.

"Do you *think* you screwed something up?" Nickie asked.

"No. I've done everything perfectly. Ben literally told me, 'Not bad' last week. But now I don't know *what* to think. I put freakin' hyssop in waffles."

"Emily." Laura waited for her youngest sister to look up. "They're moving you to another station so you can keep climbing the ladder, okay? Trust me. You've worked too hard and put too much into this to leave room for mistakes. You're incredibly talented. This is what you do."

Emily blinked at her, then all the rigidity melted out of her body, and she smiled her first real smile since that text. "Hey. You're right."

"Of course I am."

"Thank you."

"Always. That's what we're here for. Now, I have a few errands to run this morning. Gotta check out a couple...theories."

"Ooh. What kind of theories?" Nickie wiggled in her chair.

"You know..." Laura glanced at the ceiling and shrugged. "Artifact stuff." *Like specifically what I did with that dagger at the Greenbelt yesterday.*

"Did you really think she'd give you a real answer?" Emily asked through a mouthful of waffle.

Nickie snorted. "Not really. You never know."

"I'll see you guys later." Laura stood and grabbed her coffee. "Hey, if you see anything weird today, something that feels kind of off, or whatever, let me know, okay?"

Emily squinted at her. "Does the way you're being all vague and weird right now count?"

"Ha, ha. No. But I'm serious about calling me. Even if it's like, I dunno, a shimmery thing in the air, even. I'm... working on another project. I could use a few extra pair of eyes is all." Laura waited for her sisters to shrug and nod, then she smiled and headed back upstairs.

"Wait, you didn't even touch your waffles. I made them perfect!"

"Oh." Laura looked over her shoulder and wrinkled her nose at Emily. "Yeah, I don't wanna eat whatever you were feeling when you made those. Not after the hyssop thing."

Nickie laughed, and Emily rolled her eyes before digging into her breakfast—and Laura's.

I definitely don't need to be angry or nervous when I go talk to Carl about that dagger. That's for sure.

CHAPTER TEN

By the time Laura got to her room, the coffee had warmed her enough the zip-up hoodie had to come off. She draped it over her dresser and stepped into her reliquary. "Doesn't matter how much I wanna have this little chat with Carl. Bad idea to leave the house without feeding the beasts first."

Egbert the billynordle didn't stir once through feeding time, even with the squawking, grunting, flapping, shuffling, and snorting of the dozen other creatures in her magically expanded closet. She chanced peering into Inez's pen for Emily's stolen scarf. The snail-like gorlek let out a loud, warning hiss. Inez was the size of Laura's torso with a back lined in fluttering yellow feathers and a razor beak sharp enough to take off her hand.

"Okay, okay. I hear ya loud and clear." Laura dumped half a gallon of raw, chopped liver into the pen and stuck the bucket in the sink next to it. "Eat up. Calm down. I'll come back later."

Inez oozed toward the stinking meat. Her bright-yellow beak opened, and a screeching chortle burbled from her throat.

Laura side-eyed the creature. "You sound like a hyena and a velociraptor screaming at each other." She smiled anyway to see the gorlek munching away at the liver. "I'm serious, though. If you don't adjust your attitude, Inez, I won't think twice about a heavy dose of valerian root in your dinner. Whatever you did with Emily's scarf, I'm gonna find it."

Inez snorted, blowing a few soggy chunks of liver against the pen wall.

"Yeah, yeah. You talk a big game."

When she had everyone else fed, she told all the creatures to behave until she got back. "And after I get back too. Yeah, Bindo. Yeah, I know. I never leave without a hug."

A purple-and-blue-striped *kybbie* nudged his ridiculously soft nose into Laura's side. She wrapped her arms around the creature's neck. For a cross between a miniature zebra and a terrifyingly large wolf cub with two tails, the kybbie was nothing more than a giant bundle of affection. Bindo let out a few gooselike honks of appreciation, then Laura released him and whispered, "I really do have to go. Make sure everybody's doing what they're supposed to, okay?"

With a final pat on the creature's head, Laura exited her walk-in museum. She changed into shorts and a t-shirt and tucked her wand into her back pocket. She peered at the silver artifact on her thumb. "And I still don't quite trust you yet," she told the odd ring, and then headed out to have a conversation she didn't want to have.

. . .

She pulled up in front of Hopkins Antiques half an hour later. The bell on the door jingled when she stepped into the semi-dark front room filled with the widest range of antique baubles, furniture, décor, and fixtures she'd ever seen in one place. You name it, Carl Hopkins had it. He was the guy Laura came to for magical artifacts when she couldn't seem to whip up something useful on her own.

"'Morning, Laura." She glanced at the counter in the back but only saw a chipped teacup with tendrils of steam rising into the air. Carl popped his head up from behind the counter and stood. "How you doin'?"

Laura headed toward the counter. "I'm fine, thanks. Just have a few questions for you, if you're not busy."

He spread his arms, took an exaggerated, sweeping glance of his empty shop, and chuckled. "I think I can spare a few minutes for 'the' Laura Hadstrom."

Laura suppressed the urge to roll her eyes. "Thanks."

Carl lifted the chipped teacup to his lips and took a long, slow sip. "You look a little worried."

"Not worried." She leaned her forearm on the counter. "Just curious. That dagger definitely worked."

"Excellent."

"Yeah, that's what I thought, too. As a divining rod, it's perfect. And it got me through the wards I'd been trying to slip past for weeks."

Carl lowered his teacup and frowned. "You didn't mention anything about wards."

"I know." Laura dipped her head. "I didn't want to put the cart before the horse, you know? It wasn't until the dagger did its thing I knew for sure there *were* wards. And, well, I think the dagger did a little something else…unexpected."

"Hmm. What happened?"

"I'm not sure. But I have a hunch. I think." Laura sighed and shook her head. "That dagger found the wards and got me through them. Would it have been able to open up, say, other binding spells?"

The antiques dealer scratched his chin. "Possibly. It depends on what the binding spells were and how they were being used."

Laura scrunched up her nose. "What if they were being used as a sort of prison-cell lock?"

Carl licked his lips and leaned over the counter. "You got me interested, Laura, but I think I need a few more details."

"Right." She drummed her fingers on the counter, and the silver ring on her thumb winked in the light. "Do you know anything about a Gorafrex stowaway on this ship?"

Carl stared at her way too long, then he blinked and straightened. "I've heard the story, yeah. Gorafrex were witch-hunters. The one that got on this ship was supposed to have been sealed away. Beyond that, Laura, I can't tell you anything. There may be other wizards and witches that know more, but honestly, I think the information's been all but forgotten. Tends to happen with eternal prisoners."

"Yeah, I need a little more than that." Laura closed her eyes and took a deep breath. "I think that dagger is more than just a divining rod. Or I helped it become something else. I dunno. I'm pretty sure I let the magical cat out of the bag."

"The Gorafrex." The shop owner let out a low whistle and rubbed his chin. "That *would* be a sour pickle, wouldn't it?"

Laura snorted. "That's not even the worst part. My little run-in with the Gorafrex, if that's what this is, happened before I found out last night that my sisters and I are next in the magical bloodline of this thing's jailers. Protecting wizards and witches all over Earth from the thing that shouldn't have gotten on this ship in the first place. And I let it out." A bitter laugh escaped her.

"All right, now. Don't go beatin' yourself up over this just yet." Carl sniffed and took another sip of tea.

"Nope. I haven't gone that far down the rabbit hole. But if there's anything else you can tell me about the Gorafrex, I would really appreciate it, 'cause I need to figure out how to put this thing back where it belongs."

"Agreed. I'm not sure I can point you to anyone with more to say. Especially since you're part of the family meant to keep this thing where it belongs." Carl's brow furrowed and he held up a finger. "You know what? I might have something in the back. Not a how-to, by any means, but it may steer you in the right direction. Just a minute, okay? Lucinda has Sundays off, so it's just me rootin' around through things back here."

"No problem."

"Just give us a shout if a customer shows up."

Laura turned to survey the overwhelming assortment of trinkets inside Hopkins Antiques, but she couldn't clear her mind enough to focus on any of them. Thankfully, Carl took less time to find what he wanted than expected.

"Okay. It's not complete by any means, but this might have something." He dropped a giant book onto the counter with a puff of dust.

"What is it?"

"Something like a manifest. Obviously, it's outdated. And there's no possible way to account for everyone riding this thing nowadays. *But...*" He gingerly opened the cover, which had softened so much even with the preservation charm it bent like paper in the man's hand. "It *should* have an account of all the original races that boarded the first time, way back when. We might find something in here."

"About the Gorafrex?"

Carl shook his head. "Not if it was a stowaway, right?"

"Oh...duh."

"I think the best bet is to look for someone in here who might have more in-depth knowledge of the Gorafrex itself or how to put it back, as you so succinctly put it."

Laura looked up to find him smirking at her. She gave him a dry smile and they both returned their attention to the manifest. "Maybe even someone who's been here from the very beginning," Carl said. "If it was witches' magic that locked the Gorafrex up the first time, that's likely what'll have to happen again. Not that there are any witches or wizards still living now who were there that day, but there's no shortage of immortals on this ship."

"Yeah, I know. My dog's one of them."

The man frowned at her in amused curiosity.

"Totally different story."

"Okay. How do you feel about skimming through this

thing with me? Honestly, I wish I had the time to read through and memorize every volume in my collection, historical or otherwise." Carl let out a huge sigh. "But life is just too short and sweet."

Laura smiled. "Yeah, I can help look. I'll take the left pages, you take the right?"

"Works for me." He turned the book ninety degrees so they could peer sideways along the counter and read their designated pages.

After an hour of poring over the manifest—and twenty minutes after Carl had pulled up stools for both of them— Laura's growling stomach interrupted her concentration. *Yeah, feed all the creatures and forget to feed myself. Great start.* "Do you still think we're gonna find anything in here? I mean, the mechanics would be the best bet, right? But they don't...they don't really come up to talk to anybody, right?"

"Not in a long time, as far as I know." Carl grinned. "You picked the perfect time to ask, though. I think I found the immortals you need."

Laura smacked her hand down on the counter. "You have never let me down, Carl."

"Well, I do my best." He spun the book around and pointed at the top of the right-hand page.

She read the first paragraph before looking up in surprise. "I've never heard of Tree Folk before."

"Well, I imagine that's because they prefer to live in trees. Did you read the description?"

"'An elven race similar in feature to several of Earth's smaller primates. Hailing from their original homeworld of…'" Laura squinted. "I can't even begin to pronounce that."

"I don't think it matters at this point."

"True." She kept reading. "'The Tree Folk prefer arboreal homes to anything traditionally civilized. Despite this, they are known among the other elven races for their long memories, most notably with historical events and temporal repercussions.' What the heck does that mean?"

Carl cocked his head. "You're more of a scholar than I am."

"I'm an *archaeologist* at an almost entirely human college. You're the one with the ancient ship manifest."

"Fair enough. If I had to guess, I'd say somebody back then figured the Tree Folk were skilled at reading or remembering the past to predict the future. Who knows how accurate those predictions were."

"But it's a start. Okay." She skimmed the rest of the page. "Attracted to simpering melodies, huh? Pretty sure I know a witch who can pull that off."

"Your sister?"

"Who *isn't* talking about the twenty-first century's new Queen of Blues?" Laura laughed. "We just need her to play something for the Tree Folk without bringing a huge crowd. You think it's safe to assume these guys are still around? Here in the city?"

"It's worth a shot. I mean, all the other races on this ship made their way to every corner of the globe, for lack of a better phrase. If you think you released the Gorafrex, I imagine a few immortals would stay relatively close to a threat like that should anything happen."

"Right." Laura pressed her lips together. "Looks like

'anything' already happened. Hey, thanks for going through all this with me. I appreciate it."

"I wish I could've been more helpful."

"You're always helpful, Carl." Laura turned from the counter and headed toward the door.

"Laura."

"Yeah?"

"I understand if that dagger's giving you buyer's remorse. I'm happy to buy it back. At ninety percent, of course."

"Are you kidding?" She grinned over her shoulder. "That thing's never leaving my collection, my friend."

CHAPTER ELEVEN

L aura hadn't been driving five minutes when she heard peculiar drumbeats out on the street. The hair on the back of her neck prickled and stood on end. She rolled down her window. The faint drumming grew louder, coming from across the street. The traffic light ahead of her switched from green to yellow, so she slowed to a stop at the intersection and scanned the sidewalk on North Lamar for the drumming's source.

"Don't write off buskers. That's a thing here." Yet, buskers didn't play drumbeats that gave her full-body goosebumps, and they definitely didn't show up mid-air over the sidewalk, shimmering in an oscillating mass of pearly energy. The thing she'd unleashed from that stone in the Greenbelt did, however. The ring on her thumb tingled warmth up her arm and down to her kneecaps.

"Hey, don't get any ideas," she told the ring, then peered at the shimmering energy over the sidewalk. "Oh, no."

Shifting in the driver's seat, she jammed her hand into her pocket and pulled out her wand. "Dang it. Too many *people* here..." Pedestrians went about their Sunday in downtown Austin. None of them buskers, and nobody playing drums. The shimmering energy moved behind a tall, skinny man in frayed jeans and a fringed leather vest, long dark hair pulled in a loose ponytail. For how tall he was, the man moved along the sidewalk slower than everyone else, taking his time, unaware of the Gorafrex creeping behind him.

"Guess nobody else hears the drums or sees that thing. Crap." The ancient, familiar drumming beat louder from across the street, yet drew zero attention from pedestrians or drivers. It moved faster toward the man with the ponytail.

"Hey, watch out!" Laura shouted out her open window.

The man didn't hear her. Though she drew stares from a few passersby.. The man lurched forward on the sidewalk with the force of the Gorafrex shoving its energetic self into his body. Laura watched wisps of that shimmering air disappear into the man's back, and the drumbeat cut off.

"No, no, no. Not humans." Laura lowered her wand by her thigh and watched the tall man straighten. Scowling, he turned his head. His gaze met Laura's, and his eyes flashed a blink of silver light—almost blinding even from across the street. One ear-splitting crack of drums filled the air. No one noticed that, either.

"Nope. You're not gettin' *this* witch." The second the traffic light turned green, she floored the pedal and put as much distance as possible between her and the Gorafrex-possessed human.

"It would've been *really* nice to know that thing also leaps into human bodies. If that guy's peabrain was ready for action, he could've heard those drums." She slammed her hand down on the steering wheel. "Okay. This just means we need to be quick about it." Her legacy ring pulsed around her thumb, almost like a warning. "Yeah, fine. Really quick."

It wasn't safe, but she grabbed her phone from her purse and called Nickie. Her Bluetooth connected to her stereo speaker as she checked her rearview, watching for the human Gorafrex or anything else weird.

Nickie didn't pick up even after a second phone call.

Laura gritted her teeth. "Come *on*."

She threw on her right blinker and took a sharp turn into a gas station lot, waving absently at the dude behind her pounding on his car horn as he whizzed past her down the street. "You were following *way* too close anyway, jerk." Her Taurus screeched to a halt in a parking spot. Laura turned off the engine, threw the keys and her phone into her purse, jammed her wand into her back pocket, and jogged into the store right past the clerk's counter.

"Hey, there. How are you?"

"Fine, thanks. Just need the restroom." Laura hightailed it toward the back hallway.

"Restrooms are for paying customers only," the clerk called behind her.

"I'll grab something on the way out." She stormed into the bathroom and locked the door. What she wanted was the mirror that should've been mounted over the sink like any reasonable public restroom. "Seriously?"

Her gaze fell to the toilet without a lid and the shimmering reflection of the bathroom light on the water's surface. "Oh, screw it." Laura pulled out her wand and pointed it at the toilet water. "*Invenio* Emily."

The tip of her wand flashed rosy pink followed by a soft glow and a ripple along the toilet water's surface. She took a step closer, peering down into the porcelain bowl.

At the *potager* station in the pristine, industrial kitchen of Meadowlark Tavern, Emily poured a finished watermelon gazpacho out of a huge blender and into the storage on the stainless-steel prep counter.

Anthony's gonna love this. I love this. Thank god they moved me to soups today.

She set the blender in the massive sink against the wall, grabbed a plastic container lid, and admired the perfect sheen of her first soup. As a last-minute test, she grabbed a soup spoon and dipped a little into the tub for a taste. "Oh, yes." She closed her eyes and smiled, then tossed the spoon into the sink. The loud *clink* didn't even make a dent in the noise of Chef Ansler's bustling kitchen.

She returned to the soup container and yelped. Emily clamped her mouth shut at the sight of her sister staring up at her from the rosy glimmer of soup.

"Laura," she hissed. "I'm at work."

"I know…" Her sister's face rippled. "I knew you wouldn't answer if I called your phone."

Emily glanced around the busy kitchen. "If anyone sees me talking to this gazpacho, they're gonna think I'm so in love with it that I wanna be at this station forever." She frowned at the image in the tub and the view of Laura leaning over something. "Wait, are you…? Did you invoke Sister Soup in a toilet bowl?"

"They don't have a stupid mirror in here. Listen—"

"I really don't have time for this. I'm on prep this morning, and I have three more soups to make."

"When do you get off?"

"I don't know. Twelve, *maybe*."

"Perfect. I'm calling an emergency family meeting, okay?" Laura frowned. "Without Mom and Dad…at least for now. When you're off work, call me. This is serious."

"Sure. Bye."

"Wait, wait. You wearing your ring?"

Emily took a deep breath to calm herself. "Yeah. It's fine."

"Okay. This is important, though. I mean it. If it starts to tingle, like last night, you need to get out of there. Got it?"

"Laura, I'm not gonna bail from my shift just because of a *tingle*." Emily's voice almost rose over a whisper, her face so close to the gazpacho she could've stuck her tongue in it. "I'd love to ask you why you're being so weird, but I—"

"Emily, just promise me you'll leave if that happens."

"Fine. Yeah. I promise. I gotta go. Get out of the toilet already." She couldn't help but grin after saying it.

Laura sighed, and a bright light flashed across Emily's soup, which rippled with the end of the spell.

Emily peeped at the other chefs and assistants in the kitchen.

The chef looked at her with one eyebrow up. "Uh, how's it coming with that gazpacho?"

"Chilling it now, Chef."

"Okay. Double batch of cucumber bisque next? No talking to it."

"Yes, Chef."

Emily slammed the lid down on the storage container and took it to the walk-in beside her station. The cold air brought the heat down in her face.

"Laura's gotta be *the* most literal witch in the universe," she muttered, grabbing the tape and a Sharpie from the small hooks on the fridge wall. She scribbled the date onto the tape and slapped it on the container. "Calling Sister Soup in my *actual* soup."

With a snort, she left the gazpacho on the shelf and headed back to her station. "This family emergency better be something important."

Laura chanced invoking Sister Soup with Nickie, too, but it didn't go through; wherever she was, apparently she had no reflective surfaces around her. "What the heck is she *doing?*"

With the feeling that the clerk was listening from outside the bathroom door, Laura flushed the toilet, washed her hands, and dried them before stepping back out. She grabbed a protein bar and a bottled water, which would do as a late breakfast. The clerk gave her a tight smile and rang her up. *Like he didn't think I'd actually buy something.*

When she got to her car, she called Nickie one more time. Still no answer. So, she sent a text: *'Family meeting. You, me, Em. 12:30. Anything weird with your ring, call me.'*

"Guess that's good enough for now." She unwrapped

the protein bar and munched on it, while trying to think of something productive she could do for the next two hours. "I mean, there's always the library. Carl didn't suggest it, but it's not like he's an encyclopedia on witch-killing energy creatures. Worth a shot." Shrugging, she washed down the protein bar and started her car.

An hour later, Laura departed the library. It turned out the collection of magical volumes behind the otherwise normal wall in the library, which she and every other magical being could access—if they knew about it—didn't have a single anything about Gorafrexes. The elf behind the tiny help desk didn't even know as much as Carl, and Laura decided not to give the gorgeous immortal a run-down of what a Gorafrex was and why it was crucial she figure out how to catch one. The magical library was full of witches, anyway. "No need to start up mass witch-and-wizard hysteria with this."

Stopping outside her car, Laura closed her eyes. "You can do this. Find that thing and put it back where it belongs. At least I'll be able to recognize it by the tall-man body it's wearing now. Poor guy...I bet he's got no idea what's happening. Jeez, I don't either." She stuck her keys in her purse and decided to take a walk. It was muggy, but when she stepped amidst some dogwood trees beside an open space, the shade and gentle breeze relaxed her.

"I don't need my sisters to *look* for Tree Folk."

She felt like a little girl again, walking through the trees and peering up into their wide, stretching branches for any sign of an elven race that apparently looked like monkeys. "Hello? Anyone, uh, up there?"

A large group of grackles screeched from some trees ahead.

"Think any of you could tell me where they are?"

The birds ruffled their feathers, stretched their wings, and squawked.

"Or maybe tell the Tree Folk Laura Hadstrom's looking for them? I guess I'm asking for a little help here."

The messengers of the magical world either didn't hear her over their own screeching or just didn't care. She turned around and headed back through the trees toward her car. *They* should *care, though. Now that I let a possessive witch-hunter out of its cage. Nickie's music-magic would be really useful right now.*

She headed to her car and drove to Meadowlark Tavern. She figured she'd sit in the parking lot until Emily's shift ended, which wasn't much longer. "She can't avoid me this way. And if that Gorafrex comes anywhere near the restaurant, I'll know."

What she didn't know was what she'd do if it found her.

CHAPTER TWELVE

With a bare foot on the arm of the living room couch, Nickie played the hell out of her Fender Deluxe Strat. The first few chords rippled down her back. Usually, it was just sweat. Right now, it was all magic.

"You're gonna go higher than I ever did, Nickie," her dad told her more times than she could count. "Keep tapping your magic."

This new song she was putting together had bluesy funk draped all over it. Her amp against the back wall vibrated the floor, and she either sang whatever words popped into her head or hummed, grunted, and growled in place of words she'd yet to write.

"Yep. That's it." She grabbed her wand from beside her foot on the couch's armrest, pointed it at her lyric notebook on the coffee table, and wrote down what she had. Another downloading spell jotted down the chord progressions at the top of the page, and that was all she needed.

"Killin' it." She put her wand down on the armrest and

dove back in where her magic was strongest. Everything else floated away into nothing.

Just after she'd finished playing through a fiery solo— no backing track necessary—the smell hit her. Her hand dropped from the strips, and she sniffed again. "Aw, Speed! Come *on*, buddy."

For a few seconds, the only sound was the soft buzz of the amp, then came the telltale jingle of Speed's approach. The short, chubby bulldog trotted into the living room from the foyer, his tongue lolling as he panted and gazed at her. "Dude, I'd say you need to get that looked at if you weren't immo—"

A soft chuckle made her stop, and Nickie looked up from the family pet toward the front door. Chuck leaned against the dark wooden trim of the entryway into the living room, his arms folded, grinning at her. "If he wasn't what?"

"Hi." Without looking, Nickie grabbed her wand and slipped it down into the corner of the couch between the puffy cushions and the armrest. "I didn't hear you come in." She took her foot off the armrest and turned around to sit there, just to make it casual.

"It's kinda hard to hear anything when you're shredding like that."

Nickie smirked. "Laura goes nuts when I have the volume up this loud. So, full-decibel practices happen when she's not home. How was your meeting this morning?"

"The meeting went very well. I know I said I'd call you after, but I figured you might be home. Lucky me, I was right."

She glanced down at Speed, who'd taken a seat right in front of her and stared up at her face. "How long has Chuck been standing there creepin' on me, dog?"

"About five minutes." Chuck pushed himself off the entryway and stepped into the living room. "Right before you started—*man*, Speed. That smells like a medical emergency."

Nickie shot the bulldog a condescending glance, to which he responded by rolling over onto his back with a little groan, his front paws dangling in the air.

"You sure there's not something wrong with him?"

"Totally sure. He's been to the vet plenty. Perfectly healthy, stinky dog." She stuck out her foot to rub Speed's belly with her toes. *And if being passed down through my family for hundreds of years hasn't killed him, deadly farts are no competition.*

Chuck shook his head. "Man. Hearing you play is the only thing that makes the smell bearable right now. Is that new?"

"Yeah. I got some lyrics down, too." She nodded toward her notebook on the coffee table, and he went right for them.

After a glance, he wrinkled his nose. "You trying to reinvent your handwriting?"

"What?"

"I mean, I normally have to slog through trying to read your lyrics. These are…legible. The little swirlies are cute."

Nickie squinted at her notebook. "Swirlies." Yes, she'd taken to writing down lyrics with her wand instead of a pen, which apparently hadn't quite captured the look of her writing. And she couldn't just tell him her magic had done it for her. Chuck was human. Nickie was a witch. *And he only knows one of those things. I should probably tweak that spell a little.*

"I dunno," she said with a shrug. "Maybe it's 'cause of how much I like this one."

He'd already tuned her out halfway through her sentence. "Wow, babe. This is excellent. And what you were just playing... You know, I'm pretty sure Dave's gonna flip."

"Ooh." Nickie pulled the guitar strap over her head and propped her dark-blue Strat up in the corner of the couch —where it would also hide her wand. "Is this Dave, the owner of Blue Silk Records? Or Dave, your best friend?"

"Ha ha." Chuck tossed her notebook onto the coffee table and stepped around the couch. When he stopped in front of her, Nickie spread her legs so he could get closer. "Very funny." His hands slid up her thighs as he leaned toward her. "Because they're the same guy, right?"

"Mm-hmm." Nickie leaned back just enough to make him wrap his arms around her, and he pulled her in for a long, deep kiss. Then she jerked away with wide eyes, and he raised his hands in surrender. "You know, I really shouldn't be making out with my manager."

"Okay, okay. Taking off the manager hat. I promise."

"Excellent." She slid her hands up his chest to drape her arms around his neck and kissed *him* this time. Her feet brushed up along each of his legs before she dug her heels into the back of his thighs and drew him closer.

He chuckled and held the back of her head to keep her where she was, but Nickie pulled back anyway and bit her lip. *Blue, blue eyes, baby. Love 'em.*

A loud snort came from the floor, where Speed was still lying on his back, either snoring or trying not to sneeze. With a sigh, Nickie ran a hand through Chuck's soft blond hair and brought her lips to his earlobe. A little nibble on his ear, followed by a flick of her tongue, and she could hear him shiver.

"I need your help with something," she whispered.

"Yeah?"

"Follow me." She kissed his neck, then pushed herself off the arm of the couch and forced him a few steps back. Slipping out from between him and the couch, she headed toward the far side of the living room and the back of the house.

"Seriously?" Chuck called behind her.

"Oh, hey. Grab that hamper on the chair and bring it with you." She turned to point at the plastic bucket of dirty clothes and grinned. "Please."

The sound of his disbelieving laughter followed her under the huge house's central staircase. *Yeah, I'll make it up to you.*

In the mud room by the back door, Nickie opened the dryer and the washing machine to move over the rather small load. *Only Laura would do laundry for like...six things.* She'd put everything in the dryer, plus a dryer sheet, by the time Chuck caught up with her.

The plastic bucket dropped from his hands and thumped onto the stained linoleum. "Okay. I stopped talking shop. Not sure I can take off the boyfriend hat, though. So please tell me you didn't ask me in here to do your laundry."

Nickie laughed. "I'm a big girl, baby. I can do my

laundry all by myself." She started the dryer, then got to work dumping all her own dirty clothes into the washer.

"All right, babe. Do you even need my help, or were you just screwin' around?"

Bent over the hamper and tossing clothes into the wash, she looked up at him and winked. "I definitely need your help. Just give me a minute."

"Okay…" Chuck folded his arms and watched her.

With the hamper empty, Nickie stood and stripped off her shirt. That went into the washer too, followed by her leggings. Next, she slithered out of her green lace panties and dangled them on her toe before kicking them into the washer. She paused and glanced down at her bra. *I mean, clean is clean.* So she took that off too, tossed it in with all her other dirty, unsorted clothes, and closed the door.

"So…what are you doing?"

After turning on the washer, she spun around and raised an eyebrow at him. "Multitasking."

"Okay, when you said, 'Follow me', I thought you had something completely different in mind." He looked her from top to bottom and cocked his head. "This isn't helping."

"Good." Stepping toward him, she reached out and grabbed his belt buckle with both hands. "You weren't wrong."

The next second, he'd grabbed her face with both hands and kissed her with even more heat than last time. Nickie tugged on his belt again, pulling him back toward the dryer as she opened the buckle and unbuttoned his jeans. Laughing, he let go of her long enough to drop his pants, and she hopped up onto the rumbling dryer with a grin.

"Oh..." He grabbed her hips and jerked her just a little closer to the dryer's edge. "Yeah, we got plenty of time."

It turned out they only had two minutes alone in the mudroom before the front door burst open and Nickie heard both her sisters shout her name. She giggled and pulled Chuck closer.

"Nickie?" Laura called. "Your boots are in front of the door, so I know you're here. I called you like five times. What's going on?"

"I'll go check the kitchen," Emily said.

"Crap." Nickie pulled away from Chuck and blinked at him. "She's coming back here." With a frustrated sigh, he stepped away from her as she launched herself off the rumbling dryer. "Babe, I'm sorry."

"Guess that's what we get for being back here, huh?" He snorted and put his clothes back on.

Nickie jerked open the dryer door and grabbed a bright-lavender tank top and a pair of damp cargo shorts. She'd just finished tugging on Laura's clothes—which fit her but which she'd never wear—when Emily came through the doorway from the kitchen on the other side of the mudroom.

"Oh, hey. There you are." Emily stopped and raised an eyebrow at Laura's wet clothes on Nickie and Chuck's hair sticking straight up, both of them looking like rabbits caught in a snare. "In...the mudroom, huh?"

Nickie kicked the dryer door closed, which turned the cycle back on. "What's up?"

Emily grinned. "Sorry about the interruption, guys. Laura's calling an emergency family meeting right now. Or more of a sister meeting, I guess." She shrugged and kept grinning.

"How much of an emergency?" Nickie folded her arms over the wet tank top and raised an eyebrow.

"Enough to call me at work."

"I thought you don't answer your phone at work?"

Emily glanced at Chuck and cocked her head, still smiling. "I don't, Nickie. Laura called me…you know. Directly."

She means Sister Soup. "Oh. Is everything okay?"

"I have no idea. But she's—"

"What is *taking* you guys so long?" Laura's voice headed toward the mudroom from the living room on the other side. "I'm not just making this stuff up. We have a serious—oh." The oldest sister stopped in the doorway and plastered on a surprised smile. "Hi, Chuck."

"Hello." Chuck glanced from sister to sister, then ran a hand through his hair. "This sounds like none of my business. Which is totally cool. I'm just…I'm gonna go." He slid an arm around Nickie's waist and pulled her in for a kiss. "Call me later? We can finish our talk."

Nickie gazed into his blue eyes and bit her lip. "Definitely."

"Yeah." Then he pulled away and pointed at her. "Your clothes are wet, by the way."

"Thanks. I noticed."

"Wait." Laura frowned. "Those are *my* clothes."

Chuck gave a short laugh and grabbed Nickie's hand to give it a squeeze. "Whatever the emergency is," he told her sisters, "I hope it's not too bad." Then he released her and headed out. "Later, Hadstrom girls."

They all called goodbye after him, then Laura gave

Nickie a full once-over. "Why are you wearing my wet clothes?"

Nickie grinned. "You don't wanna know. I'm gonna run upstairs real quick and change."

"Okay, but seriously. I need to talk to you guys."

"Sure, Laura. I'll be right back."

CHAPTER THIRTEEN

"**Y**ou did *what?*" Nickie blinked and reached for the glass of water she'd poured herself. But she didn't pick it up to drink it.

"Yeah." Laura glanced at Emily, because Nickie was ogling the kitchen table where they'd sat for the *emergency meeting*. "I had no idea what the wards were for when I was at the Greenbelt, and honestly, I thought I blew something up when that shimmery energy thing exploded out of the stone. I only put two and two together last night when Dad told us about the legacy and gave us these." She turned up her thumb with the silver ring on it, realized a thumbs-up wasn't really appropriate, and dropped her hand back into her lap.

"I'm just wondering why you didn't tell us about it, like...last night." Emily had both elbows on the table and her chin propped up in both hands, scrutinizing her oldest sister with a narrowed gaze.

"I didn't have the chance," Laura said. "I came home to change, you graduated, we went to dinner."

"Then *you* went to bed. After trying to crack the secrets of *your* family ring. And you could've told us this morning—"

"Okay. Yes. I had plenty of chances. Happy now?"

Laura's sisters shrugged.

"But seriously, if I'd brought this up *before* I saw the really bad part with my own eyes, you both would've told me I was blowing things out of proportion and needed to wait until Dad shows us the Gorafrex prison site on Tuesday."

Nickie raised a finger and opened her mouth to say something, then huffed. "Yeah, we definitely would've told you that."

"Wait." Emily raised her head and smacked both hands down onto the table. "What's *the really bad part?*"

Laura stared at her, then grabbed Nickie's glass of water and downed half of it. She set the glass down and gave them a low breath of frustration.

"I saw the Gorafrex this morning after I left Hopkins Antiques."

Nickie folded her arms. "What were you doing there?"

"I figured Carl might know something about the Gorafrex, or at least know where to go for more information. Turns out I was right, and he—"

"Whoa, whoa. Hold on." Emily shifted in her chair. "I know you and Carl are friends. Or acquaintances with the same weird interests. But you told *him* about this thing before you told *us?*"

"Yes." Laura swallowed and looked at them. "I bought the bronze dagger from him, and since he knew how it could help me do what I wanted it to do, I thought maybe he'd also know why it did something I didn't intend. I know I should've told you sooner, guys, but...I mean, it's our family's *job* to keep that thing locked up, and right before Dad decides it's the perfect time to actually tell us that, I let this thing loose to go flying all over the city and work its revenge on the witches who locked it up in the first place. And since *those* witches aren't alive anymore, I'm assuming it's gonna come for us. I was trying to clean up my own mess before it got worse and dragged you both into it."

Emily squinted and chewed at the corner of her fingernail. "Is that *the really bad part* you saw?"

"Not exactly."

"Ooh, fun." Nickie feigned excitement.

"The worst part, I think, is that the Gorafrex kind of... possesses people." Laura spread her hands and glanced between them.

"Uh-huh."

"Like, just anyone?" Emily asked.

"No." Laura rubbed her hands together. "Otherwise, I'm pretty sure it would've zapped itself into me yesterday. Now that I think about it, it probably tried. But maybe couldn't because I'm a witch."

"Did Carl tell you all this?"

"Nope. I'm just putting all the pieces together as they—" Laura's silver ring flashed again with its own light, and she jerked upright in her chair. "Oh. Thanks for speeding up the process."

"Laura, we haven't said anything." Nickie reached for her water glass but still didn't pick it up.

"What? Oh. No, I'm just—forget it. Like I said, all the wheels are turning."

"Uh, you didn't say that," Emily added.

"Okay, stop. Both of you just stop!" Laura flung her hands out for emphasis, her ring glowed, and the lights in the kitchen blinked off. Her sisters stared at her with wide eyes, then looked at each other. "Still haven't figured out how that thing works yet. Have you?"

"No."

"Not even a little."

"Right. Can you guys just not say anything until I'm finished?"

She got curt nods, and she pressed her palms together. "Thank you. So, we know the Gorafrex hunts and kills witches. That's what it was doing on our...homeworld. And that's probably what it's gonna keep doing now that it's out of that prison-stone thing. From what I saw yesterday, and what I saw today, I don't think it can actually *do* anything in its true form."

Emily opened her mouth to say something, but Laura raised a finger. "Almost done. I think it needs a physical body to perform any kind of magic or affect anything physical. But it can't squeeze itself into a witch or a wizard, so it took a human." Laura put her hands in her lap and gazed from one sister to the next. "Okay. Finished."

"Right." Emily nodded. "First question. You actually saw the Gorafrex possess a human?"

"Yes."

"And that was *the really bad part?*"

"Yes."

"Do you think it awakened the human's peabrain?"

Laura paused. "I don't know. I don't *think* so. No one else saw this thing floating around. I think they were all humans who haven't woken up yet. And the Gorafrex made this sound, right? Like a heavy, fast, loud drumbeat. It was…primal, really. And nobody heard it but me."

"So, humans are fair game, but they can't see it coming."

"Right."

Nickie cocked her head. "And you called an emergency meeting because you want us to help you."

"Right again."

"Okay, Laura, I want to help you. Really." Nickie shook her head. "Forget that you took a minute to tell us. But I literally have no clue *how* to help."

"I need you to help me get in contact with someone who *knows* what to do." Laura nodded at Nickie and smiled. "It's actually the perfect fit for you. And I already know who we're looking for."

"That's a plus," Emily said.

"Yeah."

"Who is it?"

"We have to find the Tree Folk."

Emily turned to look at Nickie. "Do we also need a refresher course on this one?"

"I think so."

Laura leaned toward them. "I hadn't heard of them either. But Carl has this manifesto of all the races and species that got on this ship as passengers however long ago. We found an entry in there about the Tree Folk.

They're basically elves who live in trees and look like monkeys."

"Huh?"

"Yeah. *And* they supposedly have the longest memories of any other elven race. They're immortal, and the long memory means—"

"They're more likely to remember the Hadstroms who built the prison and put the Gorafrex in there." The pieces were coming together for Nickie.

"Exactly. I mean, there was also something in there about the Tree Folk specializing in temporal repercussions. Carl said he thinks it means they're just really good at predicting the future. Who knows? Maybe people thought they could actually *tell* the future at some point."

"How is this a perfect fit for Nickie?" Emily kept chewing on her fingernail.

"The manifesto said they're 'attracted to simpering melodies.'"

Nickie threw her head back and barked out a laugh, nearly knocking herself backward out of her own chair. "You've gotta be kidding me."

Emily giggled. "Hey, there's nobody *simperinger* than you."

"More simpering?" Laura suggested.

"Yeah, but less fun."

Wiping her eyes, Nickie leaned forward and fought another laugh attack. "Okay. You want some music. And this'll give us a chance to talk to them about how to put the Gorafrex back in the cage?"

"That's what I'm hoping. I'm also hoping the Tree Folk are actually still *here*. In Austin. I'm sure they are, if they remember the prison in the first place and are so good at *predicting* the future. Right?"

"Worth a shot." Nickie stood, grabbed her half-full glass of water, and finally brought it to her lips to drain it. "Ready?"

"That's a silly question." Emily scooted her chair noisily backward and jumped to her feet.

"Oh, just one more thing." Laura stood with them and wiggled her right hand with the silver ring on her thumb. "When I saw the Gorafrex this morning, I got the same tingly feeling from my ring. You know, the same as when we all put them on last night. I mean, we'll be together now, but just in the future. Just in case. If your ring starts tingling, I think that's a pretty accurate indicator that our escaped prisoner is somewhere close by."

"That's what you meant?" Emily asked.

"Yeah. But you were busy."

"Wait, when did you guys talk?" Nickie pointed back and forth between them.

"When Laura Sister Souped me at work, remember? She literally appeared in the soup."

"Seriously?"

Laura grinned. "Gazpacho, right?"

"Thankfully, it did *not* change the flavor."

Laughing, Nickie shook her head and went through the mudroom to the living room. "I'm gonna go acoustic for this, I think."

"Excellent." Her sisters followed suit, and Emily looked at Laura over her shoulder. "Let's hunt down this witch-hunter, huh?"

CHAPTER FOURTEEN

With guitar case in tow, Nickie led them out of their house on Pressler Street and toward Laura's Taurus, the only car parked in front of the house.

"Shotgun." Emily skipped down the steps on the hill.

"Whatever."

"Wait a minute." Laura looked around at the empty curb and driveway. "Em, how'd you get to work?"

Her youngest sister shrugged. "Uber. But if you wanna take me back by campus after Nickie's played her private show for the tree elves, that'd be cool." Emily skipped down the last of the steps and stopped at the passenger-side door.

"Yeah, I can do that. And *you* can drive next time."

"Sweet."

They piled into the Taurus, and Laura drove slowly down Pressler Street to head toward West 6th.

"Did Carl tell you where to find these Tree Folk?" Emily asked, staring out the passenger window.

"Not really. Just that they live in the trees. I'd thought

we'd start at something like Waterloo Park or down by the river and kinda work our way through Austin, maybe."

Nickie chuckled. "It's foolproof."

"I'm working with what I've got, okay?"

"I know you are. That's just a lot of space to cover."

"Well, if these Tree Folk are so *attracted* to music it was important enough to add to their description in Carl's old book, hopefully some really good music will be enough to get their attention."

"Plenty of good music in this city," Nickie said. "Why haven't we heard of them before? They should be all over."

"Uh, duh." Emily turned around in her seat to wiggle her eyebrows at Nickie. "Not regular Austin City music, awesome as it may be. The folk want really good *magical* music."

"I'll do my best, guys. Hey, can you turn up the air?"

Laura reached for the dash then stopped. "It's already on."

"It's really hot back here." Nickie fanned her face with a hand, then saw the cause of heat with AC. "Oh. Laura, your window's open."

"What? Oh, right. Sorry. I rolled it down earlier when I heard the—"

"Look out!"

"*What?*" Laura slammed on the brakes when Emily's hand shot out to grip the oldest Hadstrom sister's thigh. All three of them lurched against their seatbelts, but Laura had stopped the car in time to avoid running over a massive group of grackles standing in a chaotic gathering in the middle of the street. "What the heck are they *doing?*"

"Not moving, apparently." Emily removed her hand from her sister's leg.

Nickie peered through the windshield from the backseat. "Birds normally get out of the way. This is freaky."

Laura pressed lightly on her car horn a few times. The soft honks made a few of the closest grackles ruffle their feathers and hop back a few inches, but that was it. "This is nuts. We're trying to get somewhere." She slid her finger onto the automatic window button to roll it up the rest of the way.

"Wait, wait. Leave the window down." Emily nudged her oldest sister and held up a hand. She cocked her head and stared at the dashboard. "Do you guys hear that?"

"Mm, I hear a whole lotta squawking blackbirds," Nickie said.

"What are we listening for?" Laura asked.

"Just...the squawking." Emily looked at her sisters. "Hear it now?"

"Come."

"Come, come."

Laura laughed and smacked the steering wheel. "They heard me." Of course, it was one more thing her sisters didn't know, so she grinned and gripped the steering wheel tighter. "I tried to find the Tree Folk earlier. Obviously, I don't have any kind of musical talent, but I did tell a tree full of grackles I was trying to get in touch with them."

"You ever hear one of these birds actually talk before?" Emily asked.

"Nope."

Nickie shrugged. "Just once. A long time ago." Her sisters stared at her. "Hey, it was just once. Summer after sixth grade, I think. I was writing music in the backyard and I got frustrated because it wasn't coming to me, so I threw my notebook. Then this big old bird came down and told me not to give up. I kid you not."

Emily grinned. "It was 'Something Deep", wasn't it? The song."

"Yeah! "Something Deep". Good call, Em."

Laura's jaw dropped. "Wait, you're telling me your debut single was inspired by one of *these* things?"

"No. More like encouraged."

They shared a laugh until Emily looked back through the windshield. "Oh, hey." She flapped a hand at Laura's arm. "They're moving. Follow those birds!"

Laura snorted. "Already on it, you goon."

Emily smirked and sat back in the passenger seat. "I'm feeling a *Wizard of Oz* joke in here somewhere."

"Don't." Nickie and Laura said it at the same time, and Emily burst out laughing. Still, it didn't keep her from shouting out the general direction of the grackles moving in front of them. Half the birds hopped across the asphalt while the other half flew ahead, playing a kind of rotating leapfrog with wings until they came to Springdale Road. Then, the entire flock lifted at the same time and took off flying.

Laura came to a stop sign and braked.

"What are you doing?" Emily gestured toward the massive cloud of grackles. "You have to follow them."

"It's a stop sign. I can't just drive wherever I want after a bunch of birds."

"Yeah, I think we'd have a hard time losing track of them like that." Nickie nodded through the windshield, where the grackles were darting and flapping around in the air over the other side of the street. "Or maybe they're waiting for us to follow."

"That would be convenient, wouldn't it?" Emily laughed, and the birds' caws beckoning the Hadstrom sisters to follow didn't let up. "Let's hope the birds don't end up leading us to a huge neon sign that says, 'You'll never fix this.'"

Laura slowly turned her head to stare at her sister. "That's not even a thing."

"You don't really *know* that, though, do you?

Nickie cracked up in the backseat.

"I'm kidding, okay?" Emily nudged Laura's shoulder with a playful fist. "Boy, Laura. You look like…like you just saw your sister's face in a tub of gazpacho."

"Okay, I get it. I won't call you at work." Pressing her lips together through a smile, Laura rolled her eyes and crossed the intersection.

The grackles were hard to miss. Some traffic slowed to watch the blackbirds acting crazier than usual. Pedestrians stared, but nobody saw the flock led a silver Ford Taurus along the way.

Laura followed the birds through the other side of downtown Austin. They took her to an area she didn't visit much anymore. She snorted. "Of course."

"Yeah, of *course*." Emily tossed her hands up and chuckled. "What did you just realize now?"

"Of course these crazy magical messengers would take us to the East Side. Where else would the Tree Folk get exactly what they want all the time?"

Emily smacked her lips a few times, thinking. "Oh!" She

snapped with both hands and shot Laura the guns. "'Cause of all the musicians we were talking about. Guess they like mundane music after all."

Nickie shook her head. "You guys are ridiculous. I wonder how close these Tree Folk live to Dad. Hey, did you ever call *him* about our little Gorafrex problem?"

"No. We're not telling Dad."

"Why not?" Emily wrinkled her nose. "He was literally one of the prison guards. All the way up 'til Nickie put on the black ring."

"Laura, I agree. Dad might know something that could help us."

"Okay, sure. Dad probably knows a lot about the actual rings. Maybe even how to use them. Why they do things without warning." Laura glanced into the rearview mirror and nodded at Nickie. "But our family's been telling the same story for who knows how many generations. And who knows how many times the facts have been diluted? I bet a bunch of stuff's been left out. The Gorafrex was captured so long ago, I don't think Dad, Uncle Mark, *or* Aunt Julie were told anything about what could help us. I even asked an elf in the magic room at the Austin Library, and she had absolutely no idea what a Gorafrex even was."

"Huh." The corners of Emily's mouth pulled down. "The perils of living indefinitely on a massive spaceship."

Laura just shook her head.

"You don't think Dad would be a good resource at all for this?"

"Nickie, I don't wanna get him involved, okay? They passed the legacy to us. It's our responsibility now. Not anyone else's. There's a reason the rings stayed in our family. We're the ones meant to do this, and we *will*. Plus, I don't want to make Dad feel like he has to swoop in and save the day every time we hit a snag, you know?"

Nickie stared at her sister's reflection in the mirror, but Laura kept her eyes on the road and the birds. "You know," Nickie said, "asking for help doesn't mean you've failed at something."

"Yeah, I know."

The car was silent for the next few minutes until Laura followed the grackles into the parking lot of Bogey Creek Greenbelt. The Taurus rolled slowly across the asphalt, and the birds landed in a giant swarm on the grass in front of them. Thankfully, they were the only people here on a late Sunday afternoon. The birds would've drawn a crowd for sure. They parked and Laura turned off the engine. The three witches unbuckled and got out.

The grackles hopped about, cawing and yelling. The minute Laura stepped foot onto the grass, the entire flock burst into the air, shrieking and whipping up a gust of wind. They fluttered into the trees and disappeared.

Nickie and Emily stepped up beside her. "Looks like we're gonna have to find the Tree Folk on our own from here," Nickie said.

"I mean, at least the birds narrowed it down for us." Emily gave them a shrug.

"Maybe I can narrow it down the rest of the way." Nickie lifted her guitar case and nodded toward the trees where the grackles had vanished.

"Let's go."

CHAPTER FIFTEEN

"Man, it's so much better in the shade." Emily closed her eyes and tilted her head back, letting the soft breeze wash over her as sunlight filtered onto her face through the flickering leaves.

"Oh, yeah. Now we're getting comfy." Nickie set her guitar case on the warm grass and kicked off her boots to walk in bare feet.

"What are you doing?" Laura asked.

"Gettin' comfy." Nickie squatted beside the case to take out her Gibson acoustic, then she closed the latches and picked it up by the handle. "You mind carrying this for me?"

Laura blinked. "Yeah, sure." She took the case, which wasn't actually that heavy when empty, and caught her sister staring at her still. "What?"

"What about my shoes?"

"Ew. No. You don't even wear socks."

"They don't stink or anything."

"I got 'em." Emily skipped toward Nickie and grabbed

both brown leather boots in one hand. "Let's hear it then, Pied Piper Hadstrom."

"Ha, ha. I wouldn't be comparing these Tree Folk to rats right now, if I were you." With a devious grin, Nickie looped the guitar strap over her head, took a few seconds to tune the strings, then pulled her favorite lime-green Fender pick from the front pocket of her skinny jeans. With an exaggerated first step, she moved through the trees and strummed something light in a minor key.

Emily sidled up to Laura and leaned toward her. "They won't be able to resist."

Laura smiled. "I hope there aren't any people out here right now who can't resist it, either. I don't think the Tree Folk are gonna show themselves if there's a crowd trailing after her."

"Don't worry. I'm great at distractions."

The oldest Hadstrom sister snorted. "Can't argue with you there."

If it hadn't been almost ninety-five degrees, it would've been a pleasant stroll through the park with their own private concert. Nickie's gentle playing filtered through the trees; branches bent and swayed above her, as if her music touched the leaves as she passed. Laura studied the branches, looking for movement that might reveal the Tree Folk, but even the grackles had fallen silent. *That or they've already left again to deliver someone else's message.*

Emily swung her sister's boots back and forth as she swayed with each step. Nickie's strumming picked up, taking on her trademark bluesy tone that had taken her places. She hummed with the music, then her humming grew louder. She belted out some wordless tune and rocked out barefoot in the middle of the woods. Eventually, she stopped walking and just stood, pounding one bare foot into the grass as she bent over her guitar and played her heart out.

Her sisters watched her. "Man," Emily muttered. "Even in the middle of nowhere, she sounds amazing."

"I know. You think they'll hear her? This isn't exactly Gruene Hall."

"Oh, they'll hear it."

The music cut off, followed by a sharp, "Oh!" from Nickie.

"You okay?" Laura called, dropping the case to go see. "What hap—oh."

Nickie stepped back for a better view of the dark face peering down from an upper branch. "I didn't know you were there."

The face was both human-looking and resembled a spider monkey. Tufts of gold hair bristled outward from the male's cheeks; his ice-blue eyes lined with lighter skin than the rest of his face. The same golden hair fell down around his shoulders, and hairless, well-tanned arms and legs protruded from a dark-green bodysuit. His bare feet dangled off the side of the branch, where more gold hair sprouted from their tops just behind his toes.

The first of the Tree Folk to reveal themselves smiled down. "That was quite good."

"Well, thank you." She grinned. "I can keep playing, if you want."

Laura opened her mouth to protest, but the tree-dwelling elf shook his head. "Another time, perhaps. There's a conversation to be had and a mistake to correct, I believe." He dipped his head toward Laura and smiled. "We know what happened."

"I can explain what I—"

"No need." The elf rolled sideways off the branch and caught himself on another below it. "We hold no ill will against you, witch. Ignorance is not a crime. An unwillingness to set things right might be considered punishable, *but...*" He scratched his head. "You are obviously willing. We appreciate that."

"We?" Emily asked, punctuated by a small, short-lived giggle.

The elf tilted his head and blinked. "Of course."

Branches rustled all around, and Tree Folk emerged from hiding places within the forest at Austin's Bogey Creek Greenbelt. Hundreds appeared in the branches, their coloring varying only a little, but all of them barefoot, with golden hair, and wearing the same dark-green bodysuits.

"The messengers brought us here," Laura said.

"Yes." A female elf, her features softer and less ruffled than the male's, peered down at Laura from the next tree over. She lay on her stomach along the branch, her arms folded and her chin resting on top of her hands. "We sent them to find you."

"Did they tell you we wanted to speak with you about the Gorafrex?"

"No." The female elf giggled, shaking the branch. A few leaves fluttered down to the grass below. "They saw you release it yesterday. We've been watching. And waiting."

Nickie turned in a slow circle, holding the neck of her guitar in one hand and waving slowly with the other. "We know it's on us to find it and put it back," she said. "And we will. We were hoping you might point us in the right direction."

"We watched your ancestors build that prison," the male elf continued. "We saw them contain the Gorafrex. And we know what it can do. The rest, of course, is up to you."

"Anything you can tell us would be incredibly helpful. If there's anything you want in return for sharing what you know, we can—"

"Your sister's music is enough," the female said.

"And you're welcome to play for us again whenever you like," the male added.

"Sounds like a decent gig." Nickie grinned.

The male elf put a golden-tufted fist to his mouth and cleared his throat. "The Gorafrex spent some time last night reacquainting itself with the ship. I imagine it's a bit confused."

"But not discouraged," the female added.

"No. It seeks a human host. Has it found one?"

"I think so." Laura nodded gravely.

The male elf leapt to his feet on the tree branch, bringing a round of poorly stifled laughter from the other Tree Folk sharing the tree with him. "This is what we know. The Gorafrex is rather harmless in its ethereal form. Inside a host, however, both Gorafrex and human are impervious to harm. Invincible, some might say, until the Gorafrex abandons said host. There are complications as a result of this; whatever damage the human sustains while infested, they will experience quite viscerally the moment the Gorafrex takes its leave. Do you understand?"

"They get hit with everything all at once," Nickie said.

"Correct." The female elf leapt from her belly and caught the branch above with both hands, swinging back and forth like a gymnast. "The Gorafrex's only apparent weakness is pure iron. Unmixed. No. What do they call it now?"

"Alloys," the male offered.

"Yes. No alloys. Newly mined iron is best, but anything will do, really."

"That's very helpful. Thank you." Laura nodded, trying to catch every gaze of every Tree Folk focusing on them. "Is there a way to pull the Gorafrex back out? Of the host, I mean."

"That we cannot say. Your ancestors discovered that on their own, and so must the three of you. Beware. This creature is fast inside a host. Extremely powerful. And it has had more than enough time in solitude, existing with nothing but its own rage and growing desire to exact revenge upon those who put it there. Perhaps that has made it even stronger."

Nickie hugged her acoustic closer. "Cheery thought."

"It is not our place to intervene," the female elf said. "Though with this, I believe we would. If there was anything we could do." She set her feet on the branch below her and leaned forward over the ground, stretching her long arms behind her from the upper branch she clutched with ease. "It would be a shame to have such a gifted creator taken from us before all her music has been played."

"Oh. Uh, thank you." Nickie turned to look at her sisters.

"Is there anything else you wish to ask?"

Laura met Nickie's gaze. Her sister offered a little shrug and shook her head. "No. If you've told us everything you can about how to capture the Gorafrex, I think that's everything. Thank you for sharing as much as you have."

Lips pressed together, the male elf chuckled through his nose. "We are not reclusive by nature, you understand. And we like witches." A few of the other Tree Folk whooped, and the echo of it spread through the others gathered in the trees. "This ship has grown too crowded and too loud since we came aboard." Someone, somewhere, screeched with laughter. The male elf grinned. "Despite this, Austin is a lovely place. Especially when the music comes right to us."

More laughter and cheers rose from the other elves, and the trees shook with so many bare feet jumping up and down and so many fur-tufted hands pulling on the branches. Nickie laughed despite herself. "Now *this* is a standing ovation."

The noise died down, making the forest radically quiet in comparison. The Tree Folk stared at the witches with ice-blue eyes, a few swaying side to side where they stood or sat or lounged.

"Well, thanks for your time." Laura nodded at her sisters and started to turn away.

"I have one more question," Emily said, squinting up into the trees.

"Ask it, young witch."

She pointed toward the closest tree elf. "Do you guys have opposable thumbs on your feet, too?"

A dark shape dropped from the branches above her and dangled. A younger-looking elf, his golden hair falling in a curtain below his head, grinned upside-down at Emily and wiggled his fingers.

She jumped back, gazed at his feet wrapped around the tree branch, and laughed. "Excellent."

The elf in front of her giggled, and it was wildly contagious.

Grinning, Emily turned and nodded at Laura.

Laura rolled her eyes, pausing long enough to pick up her sister's guitar case. Nickie laughed with the Tree Folk, too, and hundreds of gleeful voices followed them through the woods until they'd reached the edge of the trees.

CHAPTER SIXTEEN

After a short stop at the University of Texas campus so Emily could pick up her car, Laura drove Nickie back to their house. Before they'd shut the front doors after getting out of the silver Taurus, Emily's slate-gray Honda Civic barreled down Pressler Street and came to a screeching halt at the curb. Emily hopped out of her car and cocked her head at her sisters. "You guys didn't have to wait for me *by the car*."

"We just pulled up," Laura said. Nickie opened the back door to grab her guitar case, chuckling and shaking her head. "I dropped you off on the street. How did you get here so fast?"

"Um…because I don't drive like a grandma."

"What?"

Nickie snorted and passed them to head up toward the front door. "Everyone drives faster than you, Laura."

"Except other grandmas." Emily put a reassuring hand on her oldest sister's back and nodded before heading up the stairs after Nickie.

"I drive the speed limit."

"Okay…"

Laura followed them inside, muttering about traffic laws and defensive driving. Nickie set her guitar case against the wall, then sat on the arm of the couch and flipped backward over it, throwing her hands up over her head. Her bare feet dangled in the air over the armrest. "Think I left my boots in your car."

"I'm hoping you meant it when you said they didn't smell." Laura slumped into the armchair as Speed clicked through the dog door leading into the mudroom from outside. The bulldog trotted into the living room, tongue lolling, and plopped down on the wood floor as Emily corrected herself so she wouldn't step on the center of his back.

"Speed, could you not—whoa." She stumbled over him and turned around to raise an eyebrow. The dog had already closed his eyes, ignoring her completely. Pulling the ottoman away from the other armchair and more toward the coffee table, Emily then climbed up onto it and crossed her legs beneath her. "So. Tree Folk, right?"

"Opposable thumbs?" Laura pursed her lips. "*That* was your only question?"

"What? You covered all the important ones."

"Em, how is that important?"

"I just wanted the full picture. Like maybe the Tree Folk are *the missing link*, you know? Thought you might be interested in that."

"That's anthropology. I'm—"

"An archaeologist. I know." Emily nodded and grinned.

"I'm just messing with you. I asked about their feet out of pure curiosity, okay?"

"I like those tree elves." Nickie put her hands behind her head, her knees still hooked over the arm of the couch.

"Yeah, and they *really* like you."

"Maybe I'll go play for them when I'm not booked. You know, get in the extra practice in front of a *wild* crowd." Nickie snorted at her own joke, and Emily's giggle built on top of it until they were both hooting with laughter.

"I honestly don't get the humor with you two some-times." Laura leaned back in the armchair, crossed one leg over the other, and stretched her arms out on the armrests. "Anybody else think we should focus on what the Tree Folk told us and get to work with, oh, you know, stopping a super-powerful Gorafrex that possesses humans, puts them in serious danger, and wants to kill us and all the other witches and wizards it can get its hands on?"

"Its *nonexistent* hands." Emily pointed at Laura and nodded.

"Figurative hands, yeah. Why aren't you guys taking this seriously?"

"We are taking it seriously!" Nickie drew her legs back over the arm of the couch and propped herself up on the cushion. "We are. But sometimes, the only way to handle something super serious is to goof around a bit."

"Yeah." Emily's smile faded. "Like how Grandma used to sit outside on the porch, all day, even in like a-hundred-and-fifty-percent humidity. As long as she had the iced Arnold Palmer in her hand, she said she *preferred* the heat."

"I dunno." Laura looked affected. "That Arnold Palmer was half bourbon there toward the end."

Her sisters burst out laughing again, and Laura joined them.

"See?" Emily slapped her thighs and grinned. "You feel better after making a grandma joke, don't you?"

Laura rolled her eyes. "Okay. Any ideas where to start after what the Tree Folk told us?"

"Iron sounded like a good thing." Emily glanced between her sisters. "I'm down to just roll up wherever I go, packin' iron weapons."

"Yeah? Where are you gonna keep it? You gonna get a dagger sheath and string it on your belt?"

"First of all, I don't wear belts. And, second of all, I didn't say anything about a dagger. I wanna rock a mace. Pure iron mace."

"What?" Laura laughed. "Who uses a mace?"

"Hawkgirl." Emily nodded, but her smile faded when both her sisters shot her clueless looks. "Seriously? Nothing?" Laura pressed her lips together, and Nickie shrugged. "Man. Jeremy would've gotten it."

"Yeah, what was going on with you and him yesterday... what?" Laura glanced at Nickie, who slowly shook her head.

"Uh, the only thing I need to say about Jeremy is that he has absolutely nothing to do with the Gorafrex." Emily made a goofy face and shrugged. "So how 'bout we get back to iron weapons?"

"Okay. Anybody have any miner friends? Dig us up lots of iron real quick?"

Nickie sat up straight in the couch and widened her eyes. "We could ask *Gilroy*."

"What?"

"Yes!" Emily leapt from the couch. "When was the last time we asked him anything, huh? When life started getting boring, that's when. We got jobs, we got busy, we stopped asking questions."

"No." Laura shook her head. "I'm not asking that stiff chunk of rock anything."

"Good one."

"I wasn't joking. He's a jerk."

"Which makes it hilarious," Nickie added. "The guy's a wealth of information, Laura. And he forces you to think outside the box. By *you*, I mean like the general you. All of us."

"Oh, my god." Emily doubled over with a soundless laugh, then straightened and gasped for air. "Remember that time you asked him how much a ton weighed in pounds?"

Nickie giggled.

"Yeah." Laura shot her youngest sister an unamused glance. "He told me to go pull out the scale and see for myself."

"Ha! Priceless!" Emily waved her arm toward the foyer. "Let's go."

"This is gonna be the least helpful thing ever."

"Come on." Nicki stood from the couch and stepped toward the armchair to offer Laura her hand. "At the very least, we'll figure out whether or not we're asking the right questions in order to find this Gorafrex. That's what he's for."

"Well, either that or making little girls cry for a week straight." Even though that made Nickie laugh, Laura still took her sister's hand and let Nickie pull her to her feet.

"But we're not little girls anymore, are we?"

"Thank god for that."

"To the bust!" Emily stood in the foyer, her finger lifted in the air as she struck a heroic pose and waited for her sisters. The living room walls trembled with a low groan. "Whoa, whoa. Come on. Hurry up before I *lose* you." She waved them closer, and the other Hadstrom sisters picked up the pace.

They leapt into the foyer just before the living room walls closed in and disappeared, shutting the sisters off from that part of the house. The smaller dining room left of the kitchen spun in circles, then split and elongated into two branching hallways. The staircase groaned and broke in half up the entire length; each stair flattened and flipped open, over and over until they'd melted together to create another series of walls and rooms within the Hadstrom residence.

"Okay, take a guess," Emily said. "I'm gonna go with either the forge…or the potions lab."

"Hmm." Nickie stroked her chin. "I say the basement. Dark, dry, dusty. Perfect environment for quick and stinging wit."

"How 'bout a rubble heap?" Laura wobbled her head and rolled her eyes.

Her sisters laughed, then the walls of their house, except for the foyer where they stood, stopped moving, and they were left with two options: the hallways on their left, or the short, single door in front of them that had replaced the staircase.

"Huh. No points for anyone." Emily shrugged.

"Yeah, the mirror room didn't even cross my mind."

Laura shot her sisters an exasperated glance. "He's probably in there *admiring* himself from every ancient, dusty angle. Come on." She set off toward the door with the tiny, two-inch mirror mounted in the center. Nickie and Emily followed close behind.

On the other side of the door, a giant room with an incredibly low ceiling stretched out in front of them; it was much bigger than the widest measurement of the house, but that only mattered on the outside. Mirrors lined all four walls and filled every inch of space, including the back of the door when it shut behind them and the ceiling overhead. Thousands and thousands of mirrors of different shapes and sizes, framed and unframed, warped and level, strikingly brilliant, others covered in dust and streaks of grime.

"You know, I thought we'd hit the jackpot when mom showed us *her* family heirlooms," Nickie said, turning as they stepped inside and catching her reflection on every surface but the floor beneath her.

"Right now, I'm not so sure Dad's family legacy is much better than this." Laura scanned the room; while there was nothing in it but mirrors, it was difficult to orient oneself when a thousand different versions of everything reflected off everything else.

"There he is." Emily's smile bloomed on her face. She pointed across the room at the pedestal in front of a six-foot mirror—the height of the room itself—with a thick, bright-red frame.

"Gilroy," Laura called, stepping toward the pedestal.

The sound of grinding stone echoed against every

mirror, making it startlingly loud. The pedestal turned to face them.

"Trash-lover," Gilroy replied.

Laura sighed. "Here we go."

"Nah. Come on." Nickie nudged her sister with her shoulder and wiggled her eyebrows. "This'll be fun."

CHAPTER SEVENTEEN

"Let me guess. You're here to prove *again* how much you don't know." The grinding-stone sound quieted when the marble bust of a man with short-cropped hair and a sharp, aquiline nose spoke. Gilroy's stone lips moved gracefully, but his biting remarks were never as smooth.

"Isn't that the point of your existence?" Laura asked, stopping in front of the pedestal and folding her arms. "To answer people's questions with what they *don't* know?"

Gilroy lifted an eyebrow carved in great detail. "Is that seriously your first question?"

Laura rolled her eyes and glanced at Nickie. "See?"

"He's never gonna change, Laura." Nickie smiled and shook her head. "That part's on us. So let's get crackin', huh?" She faced the statue that had been in their family for longer than anyone could say. "Hi, Gilroy."

"Greetings, you dirty hippie."

Nickie glanced at her bare feet and laughed. "Off to a great start. Hey, what do you know about the Gorafrex?"

"What *don't* I know about the Gorafrex?" Gilroy stuck out his stone tongue and blinked.

"Okay, Gil." Emily leaned toward him. "Where's the best place for us to find the iron we need to take it down?"

"Every living thing on this scrapheap has been bopping around in space for this long in a literal *spaceship*, and you come to me to ask *that* question. Ha!"

The youngest Hadstrom sister rubbed her hands together and sucked in a breath. "Ooh. We're just getting started, my friend."

"What's the best type of weapon for getting the Gorafrex into its prison?" Nickie asked.

Gilroy blinked. "You literally answered your own question."

"Okay. Let me rephrase. What's the best shape for an *iron* weapon to take if we want to subdue and capture the Gorafrex?"

The bust shrugged. "Doesn't matter."

"There! See?" Nickie turned to Laura and grinned. "Straight answer."

Emily laughed. "Question number five. I think that's a new record."

"Great. We've only wasted four-fifths of our time." Laura pressed her lips together and scowled at the stone encyclopedia. "Do we use the weapons on the Gorafrex when it's inside a human host," she swallowed, "or when it's in its true form?"

"Hit it with a slingshot, for all I care."

Laura blew out a long, slow breath to keep her irritation under control.

Emily shrugged. "Okay, how 'bout this?"

"Yeah, how *'bout* it?" Gilroy replied.

"Come on, you *know* that wasn't my question. It's this. If we use iron weapons against the Gorafrex while it's in a human host, will it hurt the human?"

"Only when the Gorafrex drops the human like a used glove."

"Will it hurt the Gorafrex?" Laura asked.

Gilroy blinked at her and cocked his head. "Will the *what* hurt the *what*?"

"Oh, my god. This is infuriating." She took another breath. "If we use iron weapons against the Gorafrex while it's inside a human host, will our weapons hurt the Gorafrex?"

"That's a negative, Ghost Rider."

"Hey! Well done, Laura." Emily gave her oldest sister a playful smack on the back. "*Three* questions, one answer."

"I think having grown up since the last time we played this game makes a serious difference." Nickie studied the bust on the pedestal with a confident smirk. "So how do we get the Gorafrex out of a host?"

Gilroy smacked his stone lips and rolled his eyes. "Well...how does someone get you out of your clothes?"

Nickie threw her head back and laughed. "Depends on who's trying to get them off."

"Nickie..." Laura frowned.

"I'm just sayin'. If we're talking about Chuck, the answer's 'however he wants'. Anyone else?" Nickie shrugged. "I have no problem punching an idiot where it hurts."

"You wouldn't actually punch someone."

Nickie raised an eyebrow. "I *have* actually punched

someone. But that's not what we're here to talk about, is it?"

"Right." Laura turned back to the bust. "I'm guessing the whole 'depends who it is' part comes into play. So, Gilroy, who's the specific person who can pull the Gorafrex out of a host so we can lock that thing up again where it belongs?"

The bust cleared his throat, then pursed his lips. "No one."

"What?" She peered at her sisters, but Nickie and Emily were just as clueless.

"That sounds like a straight answer," Emily said. "But that doesn't make any sense. It's been our family's job to keep that thing inside the prison. And our ancestors put it there in the first place. So...Gilroy, *can* the Gorafrex be captured and locked up again?"

"Abso-freakin-lutely."

"I feel like we're going in circles." Laura shook her head. "The only new thing we've learned is that we have to pull the Gorafrex out of the human I saw it possessing *before* we can use the iron. And then what? We just compel it back into the stone? March it through Austin to the Greenbelt? Can't exactly put the thing in chains and carry it away if it doesn't have a body."

"Like walking a cat on a leash," Gilroy quipped.

Laura spun and jabbed a finger at him. "You're not helping."

"Well, I think I know where we can find the iron, at least." Emily spread her arms and smiled, like she was revealing some grand prize. "Gilroy, did you mean we could find pure iron pretty much everywhere?"

"Bingo!"

"Bingo." Emily shot the bust a conspiratorial wink.

"So how do we go out looking for iron?" Nickie frowned.

"What about wrought iron?" Emily raised her eyebrows.

"*Oh...*"

"Emily." Laura turned toward her sister with wide eyes. "You're way ahead of the game today."

"Thank you."

"I'm seeing some dismantling of property in our near future." Nickie laughed. "Better get to it, then."

"We'll come back when new questions pop up, Gilroy." Emily pointed at the man's stone head and shoulders and nodded. "You've been *slightly* helpful."

The bust offered a thin-lipped smile, then rotated on the growling pedestal to face Laura.

She folded her arms and squinted at him. "What's got *you* looking so smug?"

"Just your bitchy-resting face."

"You're a stupid rock." Laura grunted and turned away.

"Almost hurt my feelings, witch," Gilroy called after her. "Good thing you're not a geologist, huh?"

She took a deep breath and forced herself to ignore him as she followed her sisters out of the mirror room.

CHAPTER EIGHTEEN

When they stepped back into the foyer, the house shifted to take on a new shape. The stairs returned to their proper place, the dining room off the kitchen stopped spinning in circles, and the wall on their right opened up from the floor to reveal the entryway into the living room. Speed lounged just inside the living room, tail wagging at a snail's pace. He barked once, but even that was too much for him, so he flopped over onto his side.

"Aw, Speed." Nickie knelt in front of him and rubbed the top of his chubby head. "Who's never gonna be the most terrifying guard dog? You, buddy. Good work." Right on cue, the bulldog let out a burst of noxious gas, and Nickie leapt to her feet. "Well, maybe I spoke too soon."

"Oh, dude." Emily lifted a hand to wave it in front of her face, then glanced at the copper ring on her thumb and decided against it. "Hey, the back fence is wrought iron, isn't it?"

Nickie eyed her in surprise. "Inspired by the stink, huh?"

"Yeah, inspired to get as far away from that as possible. Or at least outside. We should try the fence."

"Right behind you." Nickie and Emily took off through the dining room and kitchen toward the back door off the mudroom.

Laura stayed behind for a few seconds to stare down at their immortally reeking family pet. Speed looked at her with droopy brown eyes but didn't move an inch. "You should probably come outside too. Just in case." She nodded toward the kitchen, and Speed's nails clicked against the hardwood as he scrambled to his feet and waddled after her.

In the kitchen she filled three plastic tumblers with ice water. Balancing them in her hands, she kicked open the back door and held it while Speed took his sweet time trotting into the yard.

"Hey, good thinking." Emily took two of the tumblers and handed one to Nickie.

"Yeah, Grandma Eloise knew what she was doing always having a cold one on her." Nickie took a few long gulps and sighed.

"I'm not making you guys Arnold Palmers, with or without whiskey." Laura raised her tumbler. "Water's better for you, anyway."

"Hey, thanks, Mom."

Laura raised an eyebrow at Emily.

"Kidding. Jeez, I'm kidding. So." The youngest sister turned and aimed her tumbler at the fence surrounding their backyard. "Pretty sure that's wrought iron."

"Too bad we don't have professional tools for welding

or cutting," Laura muttered. Both sisters stared at her, then all three burst out laughing.

"You know, having a project to focus on really brings out your sense of humor," Nickie said as they walked across the yard. Their house was built on the top of a small hill, but the yard sloped near the black metal fence.

"Well, we're witches." Laura shrugged and stopped to study the fence. "There's not a lot we *can't* do with magic, right? It's all the other... non-magical stuff that trips me up."

"Oh, yeah? Like what?"

Laura chuckled. "We definitely do *not* need to get into that right now. If you want my sense of humor to stick around, let's focus on the project, right? The potentially life-threatening project, where we're responsible for the safety of all the witches and wizards on this ship and a whole handful of humans, most likely."

"Wow." Nickie nodded. "Yeah, no pressure or anything. That part doesn't bother you?"

"Absolutely not." Laura glanced at her sister and couldn't understand why any of this was surprising. "If there's a solution to whatever problem we have, what's there to worry about? We just do it."

"Hey, Nike's next magical spokesperson." Emily grinned and stepped next to the fence.

"That doesn't fit the situation on so many levels." Laura pulled her wand from her back pocket and joined Emily by the fence. Nickie appeared on the other side of her, the middle sister's wand drawn.

"What, you don't wanna be on TV?"

"Not lifting weight and running and sweating all over the place."

"We're all gonna be covered in sweat soon anyway if we don't hurry." Emily slipped her wand out of her side pocket and flourished it at the intricate wrought iron fence that had been there as long as their old Victorian house. "Have at it."

Laura snorted. "*Secare.*" The tip of her wand flashed. A thin scratch appeared in the surface of the iron post in front of her. "Huh."

"Something a little stronger, then." Nickie brandished her wand and tilted her head. "*Trunco.*" The post buckled a little under her spell, letting out a short squeal like someone had rammed it with a car. The rest of the fence trembled, but that was it.

"Either of you ever cast spells on pure iron before?" Laura asked.

"Nope."

Emily shrugged. "Makes a little more sense now that iron would be the Gorafrex's weakness. Normally, this thing would've been in pieces by now."

"Looks like we need some intense spellwork to break this thing up," Laura added.

"It's pretty amazing, though, right?" Nickie turned to look at her older sister. "Humans have been building stuff with iron for a long time. Forging stuff, like this fence. Weapons. Doors. Chains. I don't know. Tools. All they need is a lot of fire and skill."

"We have a forge too." Laura tilted her head. "I guess magic's just not enough for this. Yeah, then this *would* make the perfect—"

"What are you doing?" Nickie stared past Laura with wide eyes.

Emily had taken a few steps back from the fence. She pulled her arm back and positioned herself like a pitcher about to throw a strike.

"Em—"

"*Exscindo!*" A fiery-red streak launched from the tip of her wand, hit the wrought-iron fence with a deafening crack, and burst along a three-foot span of the intricate design. The fence groaned, then the entire section fell to the grass in dozens of metal pieces. Emily pulled herself fully upright, brought her feet together, and grinned.

"Emily!" Laura shouted, then ducked and lowered her voice, glancing along the rows of backyards behind their house. "Where did you learn that?"

Her sister shrugged. "Just picked it up."

"You don't just *pick up* a major destruction spell like that." Nickie laughed. "That takes…I mean, a *lot* more practice than I've ever put in."

"Well, yeah. I practiced. Small stuff at first. But, obviously, I worked my way up."

"Practiced on *what?*"

Emily smirked. "You guys remember that kid Billy Ambrose in elementary school?"

"Please don't tell me you practiced spells on a kid who bullied you in sixth grade." Laura folded her arms and tapped the end of her wand against her hip.

"Are you kidding? Of *course* not." She rolled her eyes. "Wanted to, though."

"Wait, isn't that the kid whose treehouse got struck by

lightning? Tore the whole thing down and split the tree right down the middle?"

Emily tipped her head back for one long, slow, exaggerated nod. "Yup."

Nickie laughed.

"Why's that funny?" Laura glanced between her sisters. "And what does that have to do with Emily practicing a—oh. Wait, that was *you*?"

The youngest Hadstrom sister grinned and offered a half shrug. "I plead the fifth."

A sharp laugh burst out of Laura's mouth, then she clamped it shut and narrowed her eyes. "You said you just *talked* him out of bullying you."

"I did that too. At least, I told him the next time he picked on me, his new clubhouse was gonna get blown up. He didn't believe me at first. Never really saw him again after that."

"Oh, my god." Laura fully laughed and shook her head. "You know, you should've asked us for help before playing with a spell that powerful."

"You would've just told me to keep my head down, focus on school, and keep being nice no matter what. Nickie would've beat him up. I wanted to take care of it myself."

"Looks like you covered that one," Nickie said.

Laura snorted and nodded at the pile of wrought-iron rails lying in a heap like split logs. "Yeah, and this one too. That seems like enough to start with, right?"

"Hey, if it's not, I'll blow up more of our fence." Emily grinned and swished her wand around.

"Don't get cocky." Laura knelt in front of the iron

pieces, and her sisters joined her to pile it all into their arms.

"'Afternoon!" The man who lived in the house directly behind them stood on his back porch under the awning, sipping on a glass of iced something.

The sisters froze. "Hey," Laura called back. When she raised her hand for a little wave, a few pieces of iron toppled out of her arm. She hastily picked them back up.

"What happened over there?"

"Oh…" Laura glanced at Nickie.

"Probably just some kids trying to be funny," Nickie said. "Break a few things and make us clean up after them."

"Yeah, I heard a bunch of noise last night," Emily added. "Thought it was just late-night construction on West 6th. Now I'm thinking it was a…chainsaw or something. On our fence." She shook her head and offered an apathetic little shrug.

"Huh. Must've slept right through it." The man stared at them for a few uncomfortable seconds, then lifted his glass. "It's too damn hot out here. Sorry y'all have to deal with that right now. If I see anyone out here, don't worry. I'll take care of it for you."

"Uh, thanks." Laura waved again but kept her hand on the iron pieces.

Their neighbor nodded and lifted his glass again.

CHAPTER NINETEEN

"A chainsaw?" Laura shot Emily a disapproving glance. "Hey, at least I didn't freeze and make us all look super suspicious by not having an answer."

Nickie snorted. "Can a chainsaw even cut through iron?"

"No idea."

"Great." Laura stood and balanced the metal pieces in her arms. "So our friendly neighbor's either gonna be on the lookout for a bunch of kids working *really* hard to vandalize a metal fence, or he thinks we're completely insane."

"Does it matter?" Emily followed her.

"See, this is what I was talking about. The non-magical things that just make me super uncomfortable."

"We all have to deal with it, Laura." Nickie whistled, and Speed got up from where he'd slumped in the browning grass. The bulldog panted as he followed them back inside.

Laura pressed on the backdoor's handle with her elbow, stuck her foot through the dog door, and pushed it enough to slip through and pull it open for her sisters. "Humans don't have to navigate any of this stuff."

"Oh, right." Emily stepped through the door. "They've just forgotten their entire race is actually more powerful than any of us on this huge ship, and when one of them wakes up their peabrain, they have to deal with learning how magic's real and they've been lied to through thousands of years of false history. Yeah, that sounds much better than just having to be a little bit careful so someone doesn't spy on us in action."

"Okay." Laura waited for Speed to, as always, take his sweet time when someone was waiting on him, then let the back door close once he'd waddled inside. "Putting it that way makes me sound like I'm complaining for no reason." She got no response as they headed through the kitchen and into the foyer. "Hey, I'm not complaining."

"Okay." Emily nodded and smiled.

"Really."

"Nobody said you were." Nickie nudged Emily with her elbow. "This one just went a little heavy on the sarcasm."

"If I took it too far, my bad."

The walls of their house rumbled and transformed again; the staircase folded in on itself like an accordion and slid backward. Another wall descended in front of them from the shifting ceiling. Speed panted at Laura's feet, unaffected by the chaotic whir of various walls spinning and dropping and folding all around the foyer.

Where the wide staircase to the second floor had once been, a much narrower, darker staircase led toward a basement that hadn't been there for the house's previous owners.

"You guys don't ever wonder what it would be like to *not* have magic? Or at least to not remember it anymore, like humans?" Laura walked down the stairs first, light bulbs flickering on in front of her with each step.

"All the time." Emily came down right behind her.

"It'd be kinda weird if we *never* wondered," Nickie added, then turned to raise her eyebrows at Speed. "You comin'?" He grunted and trotted after her. "I'm always thinking about how easier things would be if I wasn't a witch. You know, like, with Chuck."

"That's what I mean." Laura stopped and turned toward Nickie. "How do you handle knowing you can't ever tell him?"

"Honestly? I just don't think about it." Nickie shrugged and joined them at the bottom of the stairs. "With some things, it's hard to enjoy being where you are if you're constantly trying to figure things out and predict what's gonna happen next. Just my take."

"Huh."

The Hadstrom sisters walked into their concert hall of a basement, which would have stretched underground into all their neighbors' properties if physical space mattered. It did have a large stage at the far end with six rows of auditorium seating in front of it, but the rest of the tall, airy room was lined with shelves, workbenches, book cases, trunks, boxes, tools, a ping pong table, and the various oddities of being a witch that all three of them thought best to keep hidden away. "When was the last time you came down here to make something?" Emily asked.

"Me?" Laura shook her head. "I can't remember."

"I tried making a pair of earrings a few summers ago."

Nickie chuckled and set her armload of iron pieces onto the workbench. "A soldering iron is a lot harder to use than a wand."

"That's kind of a given, though, isn't it?" Emily scrunched up her nose and dumped her pieces onto the pile.

Laura did the same. "I think we're gonna need something bigger than a soldering iron."

"Like a blowtorch?" Nickie wiggled her eyebrows and grinned.

Emily leaned toward her oldest sister. "A flamethrower."

"Uh…I was thinking more like a really big fire, you guys. Hot enough to work with iron so we don't blow the house apart repeating Emily's major destruction spell."

Nickie frowned. "Oh. Yeah, I guess that'll work."

"Still not time for the flamethrower, huh?"

"Not yet, Em."

Together, they stepped back from the workbench, and Laura pulled her wand out. "*Caminus.*" The wand flashed yellow, and the huge table trembled. It dropped lower to the ground, elongated a little, and the wooden surface became a stone hearth. All the broken pieces of iron clinked around against each other as they toppled into the new forge sticking up out of the basement floor.

Nickie pointed her wand at the hearth.

"Wait." Emily held up her hand. "Is wrought iron considered *pure* iron?"

"Oh, good question." Nickie lowered her wand and pulled her phone from her back pocket with the other hand. Her thumbs flew over the screen as she Googled the purity of wrought iron. "Good things magical basements don't interfere with WiFi or cell service."

"There you go, Laura." Emily nudged her oldest sister with an elbow. "That's one non-magical issue you can cross off your list of inconveniences."

Laura rolled her eyes. "Yeah, okay…"

"Nope." Nickie stuck the phone back in her pocket. "Wrought iron is *not* a-hundred-percent pure. It's got carbon and slag in it."

"Slag?"

"I dunno. Want me to look that up too?"

"No, it's okay." Laura rolled her shoulders and lifted her wand toward the iron pieces in the hearth. "I've been working on a new disassembly charm. For work, right?"

"Uh-huh."

"It was pretty effective the first time I used it. I attended this excavation at the…never mind. I can see your brains melting. Anyway, it peeled away all the debris caked on a few artifacts I recovered. You know, like un-fossilizing a fossil."

"Oh." Emily nodded. "Impressive, I guess. You think you can pull everything that isn't pure out of those pieces?"

"I have no idea if it'll work to take something *out*. I used it to remove unwanted material from *outside*." Laura gestured toward the radiating forge with a wave of her hand. "But if it doesn't work, we can always—" The silver ring on her thumb flashed a brilliant white light that shot from her hand and went straight for the iron pieces. Every bar illuminated with the same white glow, trembled, and levitated an inch or two, then clattered back onto the hearth, and the light disappeared.

"What was *that*?" Nickie asked.

"Well…" Laura scrutinized her ring, opening and closing her mouth as she tried to find an answer.

"Whoa." Emily smacked Laura's arm and pointed.

A cloud of glowing soot rose from the iron pieces like millions of tiny, swarming flies. These were followed by small, round blobs of shimmering blue and green—just a few from each bar—that rippled like shuddering drops of water as they lifted into the air.

"Oh." Emily flicked her wand toward the closest tool shelf, and a tin bucket unburied itself from all their stacked supplies and floated into her hands. She set this on the ground right beside the hearth. "Has to go somewhere, right?"

Laura stared at the floating particles removing themselves from the wrought iron. When they'd all emerged, the broken bars bore a smooth, dark-silver sheen.

"Did you do that?" she asked her ring; neither of her sisters commented on her talking to it this time. With a sharp breath, Laura switched her wand into her left hand, then reached out with her right toward the extracted blobs and specks in the air. The ring on her right thumb pulsed with a soft light, and Laura lowered her hand to point at the bucket by her feet. The shimmering, green-blue sphere shuddered, then dove toward the bucket with astounding speed.

"Watch out." Laura stepped toward Nickie, and Emily moved in the other direction. The tin bucket pinged with every pellet dropping inside, and the swarm of black specks followed behind. One final particle hit the bucket hard enough to send it rocking on its base for a few seconds before it settled upright.

Then, all fell still.

"Okay, did you know that would happen?" Nickie asked, pointing at the bucket.

Laura stared at her. "Seriously? You think I would've kept something like that from you guys?"

Her sister blinked, then cocked her head. "Yeah."

"At least until you figured out exactly what happened, how, and why," Emily added.

"Yeah, I do that, don't I?" Laura glanced at the hearth. "I'm starting to get what Dad meant by the rings making our magic stronger. But this was like—"

"Casting a spell you didn't even know." Nickie leaned to peer into the bucket. "Those look like glass beads to you?"

Emily copied her, then laughed. "Look at that."

"Hey, maybe just leave the bucket alone for a second so we can focus on this part first." Laura pointed at the shiny silver iron pieces.

"Okay, you're right." Nickie lifted her wand. "Still thinking really big fire?"

"To work with this stuff? Yeah."

"*Ambustio.*" The second Nickie flicked her wand, the center of the open forge erupted in massive flames. "Jeez." They all retreated to avoid the intense blast, and when the magical flames settled, they moved closer to see what would happen.

"I *really* wanna try my ring out," Emily said, grinning at her sisters.

Laura gestured toward the fire. "Go ahead. Maybe it'll be less weird this time watching someone else do it."

"Cool." Emily cracked her knuckles. Laura winced and Nickie laughed, then Emily extended her hand toward the heating iron and took a breath. "Wait." She peered at them. "We're just bending these things into something that looks like a weapon?"

"A real weapon would be smarter," Nickie said. "You know. Just in case. I don't want to have to wield anything against a human, but if there's some kind of physical component to pulling the Gorafrex out, it would suck not to have a sharp enough sword or whatever."

"Oh, you want a sword?"

"Or a dagger. Like I said. Whatever."

Emily cleared her throat. "I can do that. I can do whatever." She took another deep breath and reached out toward the flames. Nothing happened. "Huh." Stepping back with one foot, she tried again and put more momentum behind it. "Maybe takes a little more practice, right?"

"Not really." Laura frowned at the copper ring on Emily's finger. "I didn't practice at all."

"Yeah. I know. You're the oldest and the smartest. Just… lemme try again." Emily closed her eyes, took another deep breath, then opened her eyes wide and flung her hand out with as much force as she'd cast the destruction spell on their backyard fence.

"Um… maybe it just hasn't warmed up yet," Nickie offered.

"Okay, do *you* wanna give it a shot?"

"Sure." Nickie cleared her throat, pressed her palms together in front of her chest, and took a deep breath. Her eyes slowly closed to help focus on centering herself.

Laura folded her arms and glanced at Emily, who just shrugged.

After a few more breaths, Nickie unfolded her arms and lifted her palms toward the flames.

"That looks like you're trying to conjure fire again," Emily said. "Or like you're about to sacrifice something."

Laura shushed her.

Nickie kept her eyes shut and wiggled her fingers. Then she opened one eye, saw that she'd done nothing, and resorted to using her wand instead. "This is nuts. We already *know* how to use our wands."

"Nickie, wait—"

"*Et telum.*" A green flash of light shot from Nickie's wand, and the fire retaliated by sending the spell flying back at her. She leapt aside before the green spell whizzed past her and struck an old expanding file organizer filled with papers none of them had looked at in years. The organizer toppled onto the floor, and instead of paper, a few dozen blow darts spilled out of the dividers and rolled across the floor.

The sisters stared at the blow darts made of paper, the fire still roaring behind them.

"You were thinking you'd just turn the iron into any kind of weapon?" Laura turned around and gave her sister a sympathetic frown.

Nickie rubbed her arm and then crossed both arms over her chest. "Yeah, I suppose I got a little frustrated."

"Did the fire deflect your spell?" Emily asked. "Or was that the iron?"

"I don't know how to answer that."

"Well, we're obviously doing something wrong." Nickie

stuck her wand back in her pocket and pursed her lips. "Maybe you just have the only ring that wants to cooperate."

Laura frowned. "That can't be it."

"It's worth a shot," Emily added. "I mean, if you can't turn some iron pieces into weapons for us, we're gonna have to find somebody else who can. Pretty fast too, if that Gorafrex's still walking around wearing a human."

With a little pop of her lips, Laura nodded. "Okay. If I *can* do it, I just wanna say it's not because I'm trying to show off."

Nickie let out an airy chuckle. "Yeah, we know."

Laura turned toward the roaring fire and raised her hand. "If this is how the rings work," she muttered, "I guess I just…" She imagined one of the rods molding itself into a sharp blade. Her silver ring pulsed, and three iron pieces shoved themselves together with a clang. After a grating screech and a loud pop, a blisteringly hot shard of metal leapt from the hearth and clattered to the floor at her feet.

"Holy crap!" Nickie laughed in surprise.

"You just popped out a pure-iron dagger!" Emily added.

Laura stared at the cooling weapon on the stone floor. "Hello." She grinned at her sisters, then at the weapon. "Let's see how many more of these we can conjure up, shall we?"

CHAPTER TWENTY

The Gorafrex prowled the streets of Austin, feeling neither the heat of the afternoon nor the discomfort of its host's body, now slick with sweat. The human was a gangly thing and moved with a lanky gait even as the Gorafrex pressed it forward from within.

So long. So long to wait for this?

Another sleeping Peabrain whistled down the sidewalk. "Ben! Hey, man, how you doin'?" A much shorter human stepped right in front of the Gorafrex with an idiotic grin. "Whoa, man. Are you feelin' okay? You don't look so good—"

The Gorafrex reached out with a long, wiry hand and forced that tiny, powerful second brain at the top of its hosts spine into full awakening. A series of blood-red orbs shot from the host's hand and pummeled this human 'friend' in the chest, driving him backward against a brick building.

"Ben..." the friend croaked. "What the hell—"

"Where are the witches?" the Gorafrex snarled.

"What?"

"The witches. The wizards." The Gorafrex forced its host's blood bubbles to drive the friend harder against the wall, pinning him there. "What section of this despicable vessel do they occupy?"

"Dude, I think…" The friend struggled against the magic but could not fight back. "I think maybe you've been out in the heat too long. You're startin' to freak me out."

"And you're useless." The Gorafrex clenched its host's fist, and the blood bubbles released the friend from against the wall, only to shoot straight up and pummel the unsuspecting human in the chin.

The friend might as well have been hit with the full force of a champion heavyweight's devastating uppercut. His head jerked back and cracked against the brick wall, then he dropped to the sidewalk and lay still.

"If you're not going to *use* your magic," the Gorafrex hissed, "you belong on the ground." Then it took off again within its host, leaving behind the cloyingly strong smell of lavender.

Along with every other wizard and witch on this miserable ship. You'll all fall before me.

CHAPTER TWENTY-ONE

In just under an hour, Laura had forged three daggers, an iron lance, and two round orbs with her silver ring and the massive fire in their basement.

"What the heck are *those* supposed to be?" Emily nodded at the last iron sphere the size of a baseball as it rolled to a stop on the stone floor.

"Your guess is as good as mine." Laura squatted and reached out to test the orb's temperature. Every weapon had cooled faster than it should have after launching from the fire. She picked up the second ball of iron and rolled it around in her hand. "Might be useful if any of us played softball, but I have no idea what these are for."

"But you made them." Nickie pointed her wand at the fire. "*Restinguo.*"

The flames snuffed out in the hearth with a gasp and a little puff of smoke. Her wand tapped against the stone hearth next. "*Mensula.*" A loud crack echoed through their magical basement, and the hearth grew by half a foot, squashed itself together, and returned to its original shape as a wooden table. The sisters collected the weapons from the floor, then laid them out on the table.

"Honestly, I think the ring did most of the work." Laura rolled the metal lance back and forth across the table; it was longer than the table by at least a foot on either end. "When the heck are we ever gonna need a lance? Unless one of you is planning on charging through Austin on horseback to chase down this thing."

Nickie snorted. "I'll pass this time." She ran a finger down the handle of one of the daggers, marveling at the smooth iron and its sharp blade. "Something tells me your ring made *these* for a reason."

"You think Gilroy knows what that reason is?" Emily asked, raising her eyebrows.

"Gilroy knows everything."

"That doesn't help us when he's *the* most annoying magical object ever." Laura shook her head and picked up one of the daggers. "Getting answers from him is like picking out a deep splinter."

"Nice visual." Emily grabbed the tin bucket of carbon and slag and set it on the table with a clang. "Any use for this stuff?"

"I'll keep it." When her sisters both frowned, Laura shrugged. "You never know." She grabbed one of the iron orbs. "Looks like we have our weapons. Let's take 'em upstairs."

Emily and Nickie grabbed the other pure-iron weapons and followed their sister out of the basement. Speed huffed along behind them to crawl up the stairs. They had to wait just before the landing in the foyer so the house wouldn't rearrange itself with their immortal dog trapped on the stairs. The minute all three witches stood in the foyer again, Speed slumped on his belly between them, the house rumbled and groaned, whirring and flipping and lifting around them until it settled into its original form.

"I don't know about you guys," Emily said, stepping into the small dining room beside the kitchen, "but I'm starving. What time is it, anyway?"

Laura glanced at her watch and grimaced. "Almost two. I've only eaten a protein bar today."

Emily shot Laura a joking frown. "I made you waffles this morning."

"Yeah, and you were frustrated the whole time. That wasn't gonna help me."

"Fair enough."

Nickie hefted the long iron lance and set it on the dining room table. "This thing's lighter than it looks. Hey, I could really go for a chalupa right about now."

Emily set one of the iron orbs on the table. "You thinkin' Juan's?"

"They're open for another hour," Laura added. "Grab some Tex Mex brain food before going on a Gorafrex hunt?"

"I'm down."

"Yep."

"Okay. So, I don't know about the lance and the iron baseballs, but we should take the daggers with us at least, right?" Laura studied hers. "Just in case our Gorafrex is just walking around there."

"Shouldn't we have, like, a sheath for these or something? Scabbard?" Nickie lifted the tip of her dagger and widened her eyes at the blink of light reflecting off the point.

"Just be super careful, I guess." Emily shrugged, then headed for the front door. "You guys mentioned food, and now that's the only thing I can think about. Come on."

"Food's the only thing you think about," Laura replied, grinning at Nickie, who just shook her head.

"Cooking and eating are two very different pieces of the same puzzle." Emily skipped down the first few outside steps toward the street, remembered the dagger in her hand, and took the rest of the stairs more cautiously.

"Your turn to drive, remember?" Laura waved her sister away from the Taurus and pointed toward Emily's Civic.

Emily stared at her own car. "Yeah, okay. Fair's fair."

"Shotgun! Ha!" Nickie hurried toward the passenger-side door and jerked it open.

"Okay…" Laura laughed and got into the backseat. When Emily slipped behind the wheel and shut the driver-side door, they all paused, each of them staring at their forged daggers.

"Think maybe we should put these somewhere safe?" Emily asked.

"Yep." Nickie punched the button on the glovebox and set her dagger inside. Her sisters passed theirs over, too, and Nickie shut them away.

"That feels smarter." Laura sat back and buckled her seatbelt.

"Witches don't let witches wield and drive, right?" Emily stuck her keys in the ignition and turned on the engine.

"Em, that was one of your poorer jokes," Nickie said.

Emily just laughed, threw the gear into drive, and took them in a quick, stomach-lurching U-turn on the street.

"Can you not drive like a maniac?" Laura grunted.

"A maniac? I'm driving like a girl who wants her fajitas."

It was a ten-minute drive from their house to Juan In A Million on East Cesar Chavez Street. After the first two minutes of nothing but hot air hitting them full-blast, Emily grumbled and slammed her fist on the dashboard.

"What? Why are you hitting your car?" Laura asked.

"The AC's been acting up. Sometimes."

"You realize you live in the worst place for that to happen, right?" Nickie chuckled and leaned away from her sister as Emily pounded the dash again.

"Thanks. I know I need to get it fixed. But this usually works." Emily thumped her car one more time, and the copper ring on her thumb flashed. A spray of icy mist shot out of the vents. "What the—"

"Whoa!" Nickie cranked down the AC and aimed the freezing air away from her face.

"That's new," Laura said from the back.

Two different car horns blared behind them, jolting Emily into the realization that she'd slowed way under the speed limit on West 5th Street. She sped up, casting repeated scowls at the vents. "Yeah, new and going a little overboard, if you ask me." The mist had settled now into a regular temperature for a vehicle's air conditioning. "I'd sure like to know how these rings work, 'cause this is not the kind of magic I understand."

"I mean, we've only had them for, what? Less than

twenty-four hours?" Nickie readjusted the vent in front of her until she was at the center of the comfortably cold air.

"Laura's ring makes Gorafrex-hunting weapons in a basement bonfire, and I get overactive AC in my car? That sounds fair."

"This doesn't have anything to do with being fair, Em," Laura said. "This is about our family's legacy. However these rings work, they're obviously meant to help us put the Gorafrex back in the Greenbelt prison where it belongs."

"Oh, yeah?" Emily glanced at her in the rearview mirror. "How is my car spewing ice chips supposed to help us do that?"

"Maybe we're still missing something," Nickie offered. "Dad said the rings make our magic *stronger*. What if—*ow*."

"Jeeze!" Emily jerked her hand off the steering wheel and shook it.

"You guys are feeling this too, right?" Laura grimaced at the silver ring on her thumb.

"You mean the ring of fire? Yeah, I feel it."

"Emily, pull over."

"What? We're only halfway there."

Laura slapped the back of Emily's seat. "Pull *over*, Em. I felt the same thing when I saw the Gorafrex take over that guy's body. This is way, *way* stronger. Stop the car."

"You mean it's here?" Nickie asked.

"Yeah. Probably a lot closer, too."

"Okay, okay." Emily turned left onto Sayers Street and pulled around behind the blue and green building of a custom hardware store. The parking lot was relatively empty, connected to an alley behind a few other small businesses before leading back to another cross street. She parked in the closest empty space, and Nickie popped open the glovebox.

"Wow." Emily stared at the dagger her sister handed her. "We're actually gonna try to use these, huh?"

"We have to." Laura took her dagger from Nickie and flexed her hand. "Man, these rings can burn, can't they?"

"Let's go make them stop." Nickie raised her eyebrows, then got out. Emily and Laura followed. Outside the car, the only thing they saw was the wind rustling through the green leaves on all the trees lining the lot.

"Hold on." Laura pulled out her wand, aimed it at her iron dagger, then pointed it toward each of her sisters. "*Dissimulo*. Just so we don't look like a bunch of crazies walking around with ridiculously sharp knives, right?"

Emily frowned at hers. "But we *are* walking around with ridiculously sharp—"

"Guys?" Nickie stared across the parking lot and lifted her dagger to point ahead. "I think we found it."

Laura tightened her grip on the dagger. "Yeah, that's the guy."

A tall, skinny man in a fringed leather vest and ponytail walked out of the alley between old houses converted into storefronts. His steps were measured, purposeful, and he gazed around with a sneer. The dead giveaway was his eyes glowing an opalescent, shimmering silver, which had now spread to encompass his body in an unmistakable aura.

"He definitely wasn't glowing the last time I saw him."

"We can't just attack him, right?" Nickie whispered. "The minute the Gorafrex leaves his body, that man's gonna be in really bad shape."

"It might not be so bad," Emily said, "if you're still as good at healing as you used to be."

Nickie shrugged. "I hope so."

Together, the sisters stepped forward in the parking lot, daggers held at their sides.

The Gorafrex-possessed man took one more step and stopped. His head turned with agonizing slowness until his gaze fell on the witches moving toward him. A snarl burst from his lips.

"*You!*"

"Yeah. Hi, again." Laura lifted the dagger and kept moving toward him. "Listen, you can't just collect humans off the sidewalk like that. And you really shouldn't even be out here, anyway."

The man growled. "*But I am.*"

Emily drew her wand. "Time to change—"

The Gorafrex roared. A stream of glistening black bubbles darted from its mouth and hurtled toward Emily. She flicked her wand up in front of her and deflected the Peabrain attack with a magic shield. The black bubbles burst against it, and though she managed to pop a few with the iron dagger, they kept coming.

Laura's wand sent a minor attack spell streaking into the man's shoulder. He stumbled sideways, and the bubbles stopped flying from his mouth. "No serious damage," she reminded her sisters. "Just enough to keep that thing distracted, okay?"

Nickie circled around to the man's side and shot a few minor attacks at his feet to keep him moving. The man stumbled, and the sisters pressed in, gripping their daggers.

A groan escaped him, and the glowing human body

staggered like the man was about to pass out. "*Not enough...*" the Gorafrex hissed. "*I need more.*"

"I don't think so." Emily dashed toward him, dagger raised.

"Careful," Laura warned.

"I am."

The man fell to his knees just as Emily reached him.

Laura and Nickie closed in. The door to the hardware store opened with a jingle. All four of them stared at a woman coming down the steps, who stopped when she noticed three angry-looking women scowling down at a dude on his knees.

"Uh, everyone okay?" she asked.

The man leered at Laura, who realized what the Gorafrex was about to do.

Laura reached toward the woman. "Go back ins—"

It was too late. Pounding drums shattered the air.

Nickie shouted in pain as the black ring on her thumb seared bright-hot, the light almost touching the Gorafrex. She clamped her hands down over her ears and doubled over as the drumbeat pounded, loud, fast, and urgent. The glistening mass of the Gorafrex's energetic form burst from the man's body, rose into the air, and darted straight down into the woman.

"Nickie, what's going on?" Emily shouted over the drums.

The man kneeling on the asphalt collapsed. The woman leered at the Hadstrom sisters, and the next second, she took off running across the parking lot. Two seconds later, she'd disappeared around the storefronts.

Gritting her teeth, Laura spun around toward her

sisters and the groaning human on the ground. "Nickie?"

"Yeah."

"You okay?"

Nickie clenched her eyes shut. "Just those...*drums*. I just..." She tilted her head, blinked, then exhaled. "Yeah. I'm okay."

Emily patted her on the back a few times, then looked at the man in the fringed vest, who writhed on the ground. "That peabrain is awake now."

"The Gorafrex used his magic," Laura muttered, "so I have to agree. I think we banged him up some."

Blood trickled from his shoulder just below the cut of his vest, and Nickie's smaller attacks had put a few holes in his boots. "I can heal him, Nickie, if you can't."

"Nope. No, I got it." Nickie knelt beside the man. With a flick of her wand, she produced a large, light-purple bubble in the palm of her hand and guided it toward the wound Laura's spell had inflicted on his shoulder. The bubble settled on the man's shoulder and sank into his skin. The gash closed, and the man gasped a deep, shuddering breath. Nickie repeated the process with smaller bubbles, releasing them over the holes in the man's boots in case her spells had eaten through a little more than leather.

Nickie stood and stepped back. "They definitely have the best healing magic, that's for sure."

"And you use it better than any witch *I* know," Emily added.

The man grunted and pushed himself up. "What..." He blinked his vision into focus and studied the three women gazing down at him, all with the same dark hair and wearing sympathetic frowns. Their eyes glowed a dull silver. He blinked again to clear the image away, but nothing changed.

"How you feelin'?" Laura asked.

"Uh…fine, mostly. I think." The man looked down at his hands and turned them back and forth. "What am I seeing right now?"

"You'll get used to it." Nickie cocked her head. "Eventually."

"Wait, this is…this is way too trippy." He looked at the witches again and swayed where he sat. "What happened?"

Emily spread her arms and smiled. "Think of it as an…awakening."

Nickie nudged her in the ribs. "Careful."

"Right. Sorry. So…good luck." She turned with her sisters to head back toward her Honda.

"Hey, wait! I don't understand what's going on."

"You will," Laura called.

By the time they piled into Emily's car, the man had pushed to his feet. He stumbled a little, turning slowly and gazing at the sky and the trees and down at his own hands again in amazement.

"Like he's seeing everything for the first time…" Emily muttered.

"Well, part of him is." Laura pointed ahead. "Let's go."

Emily started the car and turned around to head out onto West 5th. Nickie sighed in the backseat. The youngest Hadstrom sister looked into the rearview mirror. "You okay back there?"

"Yeah. I just…" Nickie grimaced and rubbed her forehead. "Just a bad headache."

"All right. Hang in there. We're goin' to get food."

CHAPTER TWENTY-TWO

An hour later, the workbench in the middle of the concert-hall basement was covered in empty to-go boxes and plastic utensils. The smell of Mexican spices and tomatillo sauce hung in the air.

"Okay. Prepare to lose." Emily slapped her ping pong paddle, straightened, and belched.

"Gross, Em."

"It's a compliment to the chef, okay?" Emily swallowed and nodded across the ping pong table at Laura. "We gonna play or what? I'm ready to warm up for some brainstorming."

Shaking her head, Laura snorted and eyed the five squeaking *teezlers* bouncing at the corner of the table. "Who's ready to go first?"

The tiny creatures squeaked and jostled each other for the right to start the first match; they were the same size and shape as a ping pong ball, and they looked more like giant roly-polies covered in fur instead of a hard shell. One of them broke from the group, tucked itself into a little ball and, with a loud squeak, rolled toward her.

"Excellent." She lifted the teezler, giggling when it squirmed in excitement, and looked at Emily. "Ready?"

"Your serve. Let's do this."

Laura lifted the teezler, dropped it, and waited for the bounce before smacking it across the table with her paddle. The thing squealed with joy as it soared back and forth across the net between the sisters, and its fellows cheered it on from the sidelines.

"Okay," Emily said, pausing to hit the teezler. "So, we didn't catch the Gorafrex today."

"Not even close." Nickie's muffled voice rose from below her bowed head. Sitting in a chair just beside the ping pong table, she hunched over, her forearms on her thighs and her eyes closed against her massive and worsening headache.

"But we learned something." Laura hit the teezler back again. "Right?"

"Yeah. The Gorafrex tries on humans like Mom likes to try on clothes at the store."

Laura cocked her head and hit the round creature bouncing toward her. "A little crass, but okay. I was thinking more along the lines of what happened *before* it left the first human and decided to take over the woman's body."

"What do you"—the teezler thudded against Emily's paddle with a little whoop of excitement—"mean?"

"The Gorafrex looked like it was having trouble staying *inside* the man. Stumbling around." *Thump.* "Glowing like that." *Whack.* "It did say, 'Not enough.'"

"And the drums," Nickie muttered.

"Yeah, those too. I heard those every time I saw the thing."

"And you were fine afterward?"

"Well, yeah." Laura shrugged and swung her paddle. "I mean, a little surprised. That's a weird sound for a creature with no body of its own. Oh—" She jumped forward to spike the teezler over the net.

Emily moved her paddle just right to bounce the furry little creature sideways to the edge of the table, where it bounced off the corner on Laura's side before hurtling to the floor. Laura tried to catch it but didn't reach far enough. She moaned when the teezler bounced in front of Nickie's feet. The other creatures cheered in tiny, high-pitched voices. Nickie lifted her head to give the thing a tired smile. The first-round teezler righted itself, shook its fluffy body all over, and turned around to cheer back at its peers before rolling toward the table again.

"That's a point for me," Emily said.

"Em, I know the rules."

"Hey, just sayin'."

Laura eyed the other creatures bouncing beside her. "Next up?"

Another teezler pushed its way through. She scooped it up, winked, and continued the game. "The point I'm trying to make is that I don't think that was supposed to happen."

"What?"

"I don't think the Gorafrex expected to have to jump from the first human into the second. I think it was bad timing. Like"—she jumped over the table with a grunt to hit Emily's next shot—"what would've happened if there hadn't been another human around?"

"Oh." Emily nodded and hit the teezler. "You mean it *has* to switch bodies."

"That's what I'm thinkin', yeah."

"So…the best time to go after it would be when it can't stay in its current host anymore."

"Yup."

Emily whacked the teezler at a sharp angle across the table, but Laura was quick on her feet this time. "Assuming we find it again in that woman before it gets *enough* of whatever it said wasn't enough."

"Right. We need to figure out what that is."

"You think it has anything to do with the Gorafrex activating that guy's magical brain?"

Laura leapt to the other side of the table and barely caught the teezler with her paddle. "Probably. The Tree Folk said it can only inhabit humans. It might be feeding off their magic or something."

"Until it gets enough."

"Or until we—"

"I gotta lie down." Nickie shouted the declaration, startling both her sisters out of their teezler-pong-brainstorming match.

The gathered teezlers lifted their voices in anticipation, but their friend was forgotten and bounced off the table onto the floor. A collective sigh of disappointment puffed out of them.

"Are you sure you're okay?" Emily asked, laying her paddle down upon seeing how much pain Nickie was in.

"Yep. I just need sleep. The food didn't do anything, and

this headache is…" Nickie stood. "You guys had some good ideas. I'll see if I come up with…anything else." She waved, holding her other hand to her forehead as she turned to head upstairs.

"There's some willow bark in the kitchen," Laura called after her. "Want me to make you some tea?"

"No, thanks." Nickie sounded annoyed, so neither sister pressed further. The house rumbled and creaked above them, churning to its original shape so Nickie could get to her room.

Emily peered at the squeaking teezler at her feet, who chattered away in its own creature language and seemed upset she'd neglected it. "Hey, it's just a game." She bent down to scoop the little guy up in her hand and stroked his furry back with a finger. She glanced at Laura. "That doesn't count as your point, right? We both stopped playing at the same time."

Laura held out her hand. "Whatever. It's still my serve."

Emily bounced the teezler across the table, and the other goofy white creatures cheered her on.

CHAPTER TWENTY-THREE

Nickie stopped in the living room to grab her guitar case. It never felt as heavy as right then, and she slogged up the stairs through a fog of pain and the pounding echo of those drums that wouldn't leave her alone.

"Man, I can handle a headache," she muttered, closing her bedroom door behind her. "What is *up* with this?" She sucked in a sharp breath as the heavy beat pounded away, over and over in a rhythm she felt like she knew. Yet, it was all in her head. She could barely hear herself think.

"Just *stop*..." She set the guitar case on her bed and flopped on her back beside it. Grabbing a pillow in each hand, she clamped them to the sides of her head and closed her eyes. The drumming finished the familiar cadence and faded into the relief of silence.

Nickie sighed. "Thank you."

She dropped her hands by her sides and lay there, feeling the headache recede from behind her temples. After a few deep breaths, she thought about getting up to join her sisters again and help come up with a plan. The minute she moved, the drumbeat erupted again.

Nickie bolted upright. "Come *on*!" She barely heard her own voice over the Gorafrex's wild, tribal rhythm. She shut her eyes, and between the lulls of the rhythmic beating, she heard a loud *snap*.

The latches on her guitar case had popped open. Nickie squinted over and watched the lid creep open and fall backward onto the bed. When she pointed at it in confusion, the black ring on her thumb caught her attention with its glow.

"Oh. Great. My head's literally pounding, and you want me to pick up and play." She glared at the ring, then shook her head. "I sound like Laura, talking to inanimate objects."

A warm buzz came from the ring, and Nickie's acoustic guitar pulsed with a similar blackish glow.

She sighed. "Okay. Message received. If real music will get these stupid drums out of my head…" She slipped the neon-green pick from her pocket and crossed her legs on the bed.

Lifting her guitar out of the case relieved the headache a little, though the drums still thumped away in their urgent cadence. She strummed away with no idea of where she was going.

After about a minute, she stopped. "There's no way I can play something with this stupid noise in my head." Her ring and guitar flashed. Nickie sighed. "I don't get it." She settled the guitar in her lap again and put her fingers across the frets. She closed her eyes. "The rings make our magic stronger. Okay."

When Nickie played this time, she stopped fighting the

drumbeats and found herself listening to them instead. They had a definite pattern. Something she could work with.

Her wordless song melted into the rhythm of the drums, and she didn't even have to think about what chords she was playing.

This sounds way too familiar.

She began humming, and the melody found itself in the music. The more she hummed, the quieter the drums, until finally, the beating rhythm was gone.

Nickie kept humming. She hadn't heard or thought about this nameless song since her dad had stopped singing her and her sisters to sleep at bedtime. Now she knew that was where it came from. Finally, the drums were gone, and her slow breathing hushed like breaking surf in her own ears. She ended the song.

"That's why I recognized the drums," she whispered. "They're the backup to dad's lullaby." Her eyes flew open. "Oh, my god. What if…? No way." Leaping off the bed, she slipped the guitar strap over her head, clutched the instrument tightly, and hurried out of her room.

Headache gone, she reached the foyer and shouted, "Basement!"

The house rumbled, whirred, and transformed. "Come on, come on, come on." She bounced in impatience until the descended staircase opened in front of her. Then she skipped down the stairs, leaping two at a time. Her bare feet echoed in the stairwell until she'd reached the landing. "You guys! I just—*what* is going on in here?"

Emily crashed against one of the shelves full of random tools on the wall as she tried to snatch a fluffy white creature cackling wildly just out of reach. "The teezlers have staged a mutiny," she grunted.

The teezler above Emily stuck out its tiny purple tongue and blew a raspberry at her.

"Come here, you little—" Emily leapt and swiped at it, but the thing curled into a ball and rolled along the shelf before dropping onto the next shelf over.

Two more creatures rolled against the tin bucket of carbon and slag. In seconds, they'd pushed it all the way to the edge of the table.

"No, no—" Laura leapt toward them but wasn't quick enough to keep the bucket from toppling over with a deafening clang. The black, soot-like particles and green-blue beads that had cooled into something like glass spilled from the bucket, bouncing in all directions and scattering across the basement. The teezlers on the table cheered, and the other three scattered throughout the basement with shrill cries of victory.

Laura put a hand on her hip and frowned. "That's just dangerous. What if somebody steps on those and—"

"Whoa!" Emily demonstrated the peril by slipping on the tiny beads as she headed toward the table. She crouched and threw her arms out to keep from falling on her face. Her palms smacked the stone floor, and with a huge sigh, she hung her head to catch her breath. "Okay. Maybe we need to find another brainstorming activity." Emily pushed to her feet and kicked the beads out of her path as she headed toward the table.

"I'm sorry I lost focus on the *game*, okay?" Laura ducked as a teezler swooped at her from the ceiling, whooping in glee. "What is that? An extension cord?" She frowned after the tiny creature. "There's only five of them in here, but it feels like a hundred."

"I know you got lost in putting all the new pieces together. But I—hey!" Emily tripped again and turned to glare at two teezlers tugging on her shoelace with surprising strength. "Are you *trying* to hurt someone?"

The furballs cackled, tucked into themselves, and rolled away in search of more mischief.

"They get upset if we don't let them get all their energy out. I don't know how whacking them back and forth fits that requirement, but it does. So just...no more teezler-pong if we can't give them our full attention."

Emily reached the table and smacked her hands down on it, leaning forward a little. "Whew. Your headache gone?"

Nickie stared at her sisters and the mess five tiny, crazed creatures had made of the basement. "Uh, yeah. For now. I think I figured out something important about the Gorafrex." She walked toward her sisters but stopped when a teezler rolled under where she meant to place her foot. Its muffled giggle made its white fur tremble. Nickie stepped over it with a snort. "Did you guys notice anything familiar about the drumbeat when the Gorafrex switched hosts?"

"I mean, yeah." Laura frowned. "I heard the drums when I...*accidentally* let it out. And when the Gorafrex dropped into the man with the ponytail."

"Right. But I mean, did it sound familiar beyond that? Like you'd heard it before?"

"A little. Yeah. Why?"

"Okay. I might've left out the details of that headache I

had—" Nickie closed her eyes when the drumming started over again in her head. "The headache I *still* have, apparently."

"Bummer," Emily said with a grimace.

"A little. But I think it's to make me pay attention. Hold on." Trying not to fight against the pounding only she could hear, Nickie joined her sister at the table and wrapped one arm around her guitar to free her other hand. She began tapping out the rhythm on the table with the drumbeat in her head.

Emily looked at her with wide eyes. "That's *exactly* what the Gorafrex was drumming. Wait, how does it even do that, though? Without actual drums. Or hands."

"I don't think that really matters, Em." Laura's bobbed her head to the beat she'd thought was just angry, urgent pounding every other time she'd heard it. Now, though, with Nickie tapping it out on the table, it had a lot more definition. "I feel like I should know where I've heard that before."

"So did I." Nickie stopped drumming and looked at her sisters. "Okay, confession. The headache's real, but I left out the part about me hearing the Gorafrex's drumming in my head for the last, what? Two hours?"

Laura glanced at her watch. "Almost three."

"How are you not insane right now?" Emily blinked.

Nickie chuckled. "I'm not ruling that out. But…I think Dad's ring, *my* ring, has something to do with it. Like it's trying to tell me something."

Emily raised her eyebrows. "You do kinda *sound* insane…"

"Emily…"

"Laura, it's okay. Do you—" Nickie swallowed against both the drums and the headache growing in her head. "You have your phone?"

"Yeah."

"Record this, okay?"

"Okay." Laura pulled out her phone and nodded. "Go for it." She pressed record.

Nickie tapped out the rhythm of the drums. She skipped a few beats and didn't quite get it on the first round, but the longer it went, the easier she caught on. Then, she stopped and nodded at Laura to stop recording. "Now, play it back."

"Wanna tell us what's going on?" Laura wiggled her phone.

"Please just do it. My head hurts so bad, and I want you guys to get this."

"Okay." Laura set her phone on the table and pressed play.

Somehow, it started in perfect time with the rhythm pounding in Nickie's head. She gave herself a few seconds, squeezed her guitar pick, loosened her grip a little and played. For the first time in her life, she couldn't have said what chords she played in what order, just that she knew they were right. With eyes closed, she focused on the drums instead of blocking them out. Then she hummed the tune she knew her sisters would recognize.

It took them a few seconds to get there. Emily drew in a long, astounded breath and whispered, "What?"

Laura stared at Nickie and tapped her finger against her lips. "No way…"

Nickie played until the headache left her and the drumming faded into blissful silence. She finished the melody from their childhood and strummed a final chord, then let out a deep sigh and smiled.

Emily cleared her throat. "You look better."

"Thanks."

Laura picked her phone up and tucked it into her back pocket. "Dad's lullaby goes perfect with the Gorafrex's creepy, foreboding drumbeats."

Nickie nodded. "I have to admit I did not see that coming."

"For real." Emily folded her arms.

Nickie rolled her head from one shoulder to the other, grateful for the silence again. "I'm glad you guys picked up on that. It would've been kinda hard to explain."

"No kidding."

"So, I played that song, sang Dad's lullaby, the drums went away. I mean the ones in my head."

"Wow." Laura put a hand on Nickie's shoulder. "Maybe *this* is part of how we get the Gorafrex back to the Greenbelt."

"I mean, the song gets rid of the drums in my head. Which is still weird. But I think that's part of *my* magic, right? With music, just like Dad's."

"I wonder if the Hadstrom who made *your* ring played music." Emily cocked her head. "That's not just a coincidence, right?"

"I wouldn't say it is." Laura frowned and folded her arms. "Maybe you playing that song, or even just singing it like Dad is something that got, you know, passed down through the ages. Like a piece of the legacy that's supposed to...subdue the Gorafrex."

"It definitely works on teezlers." Emily pointed at the furry pile of white creatures, all of them nestled asleep on top of each other at Nickie's feet.

Nickie laughed and shook her head.

"You know, it would've been really nice if our family could've kept all this information accessible somehow, you know?" Laura sighed. "Like even a guidebook. 'This is why you don't go past the wards. There's a Gorafrex in there that you might let loose. And just in case that happens, follow these steps to put it back.'" She let out a bitter laugh. "How could everyone just...let themselves forget?"

Emily wrinkled her nose and shrugged. "I think you just hit the nail on the head...for humans, that is."

"What?"

"You know. When their tiny magical brains wake up, I bet they ask the exact same thing—how did we let ourselves forget?"

"Yeah, well, we're witches. This isn't supposed to happen."

"Our family didn't forget about the rings, though," Nickie said. "They kept that part of it alive, at least. *And* where the prison is in Barton Creek. Dad said he knew where, right?"

"Yeah, he did." A slow, revelatory grinned parted Laura's lips. "Nickie, I'm really sorry you had to have a massive migraine and those drums on loop in your head."

"I mean, it's—"

"But I gotta say you're a genius. A musical genius. The most genius musical witch I've ever known."

Emily made a silly face accompanied by a hint of laughter.

"Uh… thanks." Nickie looked from Emily and chuckled at Laura's uncharacteristic enthusiasm.

"You guys realize we have a real way to put that Gorafrex back where it belongs, right? Why else would Dad have sung that song to us every night for years? It's almost as much proof as the rings that we can do this." She blinked. "Though, honestly, I understand how the music part works a *lot* better than I understand the rings."

"Well, mine pretty much made it impossible for me not to figure it out." Nickie flipped her hand over and eyed the black ring. "I think the ring put the drumming in my head, actually."

"That's a little creepy." Emily nodded. "But rings can't actually talk, so I guess that's the next best thing."

"Who says rings can't talk?" Laura winked. "We just have to figure out what language they're using. And we're a lot closer to doing that now."

Nickie readjusted the guitar in her arms. "I don't wanna bring down the mood, Laura. Trust me, I like it when you're this excited. But I feel like I should remind you this is just one piece. The Gorafrex's still out there. In a *new* host. And maybe my music and Dad's song will help us lock it up again, but we still have to *find* it. And then we still have to test our little theory."

"Yeah." Laura pressed her lips together and nodded, then she frowned and began pacing. "Yeah, you're right. I mean, short of driving around the city looking for creepy-looking humans who *might* be possessed by a Gorafrex…"

"Laura?"

"We need to find out how to actually track it down."

"Hey, maybe you shouldn't—"

"*Or* we need to figure out a way to summon it. Like call it to us." She gasped. "Yeah, that's—"

"Careful—"

Laura stepped onto a large number of slag beads, and her foot slipped out from under her.

Emily made an impossible attempt to catch her. Her copper ring lit up with a pink light that streaked toward the floor just as Laura landed hard...on a soft cushion.

Laura blinked beneath her bum at the cushion, then threw her head back and laughed. The pile of teezlers stirred, letting out a few high-pitched snorts and squeaks, then fell still again.

Laura flopped backward onto the cushion. She looked upside-down at her youngest sister. "Good spellwork, Em. Thanks."

Emily let out a small, relieved laugh. "You're welcome." Then she gawked at the ring on her thumb. "You realize I didn't use my wand or even mutter a spell, right?"

"Seriously?"

"As the only other witness," Nickie said, clutching her guitar with one hand and lifting the other, "I can say that's exactly what happened. No wand. No spell words. Just cushion instead of stone floor."

"Cool."

"Ha. Not as cool as making iron weapons by slapping a few rods together. Or shoving an ancient drumbeat to Dad's lullaby into your head. Not to say the headache was awesome, Nickie."

"All good."

Emily raised an eyebrow. "I was kinda hoping for something a little more...I dunno. Badass."

"Oh, come on. Saving your sister from bruising her bottom on the floor isn't badass?" Laura rolled over onto her stomach and craned her neck to grin up at the youngest Hadstrom witch.

"I mean, I'm glad I did." Emily shrugged. "But it'd be even cooler if I could cast that destruction spell with this thing. Or blast people backward or something. But, so far, I have a blast of air, extra-freezing AC, and a pillow."

"Maybe it's taking a little longer for you to get to know each other." Nickie shrugged. "I mean, you're a pretty complicated witch."

"It's a magical ring, Nickie. I'm not *that* complicated."

"You'll figure it out." Laura pushed herself up off the cushion and looked around. "Man, those jumping furballs really did a number on the basement. Okay, second new brainstorming rule. Clean up first, *then* do the hard thinking." Laura chuckled, then paused. "Do we need to write that down?"

Emily glanced at Nickie, who snorted and gazed around the mess the disgruntled teezlers had made of their basement. "I think we'll remember."

CHAPTER TWENTY-FOUR

They put the teezlers away first, not wanting to miss the opportunity while the five little troublemakers were sound asleep. Of course, they woke up just enough to make a lot of noise when Emily scooped them into the empty tin bucket, which she covered with a frisbee to keep them from leaping out. She almost dropped the bucket twice, but Nickie knelt beside the gray plastic tote against the basement wall to open the tiny door in its side. A bright light spilled out across the floor from inside the tote, and Emily pressed the bucket against the plastic before sliding away the frisbee. The bucket rattled, the teezlers jumped around and jostled each other, squeaking and grunting, but they finally realized where they were and raced through the little door in the tote.

Emily pulled the bucket away to be sure they'd all gone inside, then she crouched down with her cheek against the stone floor and peered through the little door. The light in their magical pen illuminated rolling green hills and incredibly soft-looking grass. The mischievous critters bounced around in delight.

Emily squinted at them. "Don't expect to get away with that kind of behavior again, got it?"

A teezler stopped, uncurled itself, and chittered at her before turning around and wiggling its behind in her face.

Emily laughed and pushed herself off the ground before shutting the door in the plastic tote. "Those things are nuts."

"They make great ping pong balls, though." Nickie shook her head and grinned.

"You know, Em, I'm really glad you're the one taking care of those things." Laura knelt on the floor and scooped all the slag pieces back into the tin bucket. "They'd drive all the other—uh...well, they'd drive *me* insane."

"All the other what?" Emily crossed the room to start reorganizing the tools, cords, cleaning supplies, and magical hardware.

"Nothing. Totally not important." Laura didn't look up at either sister.

When the house stopped spinning and churning around them in the foyer, Speed trotted from the kitchen into the small dining room. "Hey, buddy." Nickie knelt, meaning to pat him on the head until he dropped at her feet and rolled over onto his back. She laughed. "Okay. Belly rub it is."

Emily eyed the dining room table where they'd put all their daggers when they got home from Juan In A Million. "Any ideas what those metal balls are for?"

Nickie snorted.

"What?"

"The Hadstrom sisters and their balls of steel."

Emily doubled over laughing.

Laura rolled her eyes and gestured toward the table. "They're *iron*."

"Yeah, but balls of iron doesn't sound as funny." Nickie grinned over her shoulder and stepped toward the table. "So your ring made these things."

"*I* made them. With the ring."

"Okay. But we still don't know what they do." Nickie picked up one of the iron spheres and studied it under the hanging light. "Would knowing what they're for help us find the Gorafrex any faster?"

"Probably." Laura joined her at the table, followed by Emily. "But we don't know either of those things."

Emily picked up the other orb. "Oh, hey. There's a little button here or something. Oh!" The sphere clicked when she pressed it, and a tiny door dropped open on the bottom. A thin, dangling silver-glowing thread dropped out of the thing. "Wow. That's cool."

"Maybe don't mess with it until we know what it—" Laura sighed.

"Look at this. It's like magical iron dental floss." Emily pulled the end of the string, which kept growing as she lifted it away from the orb.

Nickie giggled. "How the heck is this a weapon?" She rolled the other iron sphere around a little more until she found the button. "Hey, this one doesn't work."

"Laura, do you make us a dud weapon?"

Laura snorted, picked up a dagger, and pretended to study it. "My ring made those, okay?"

"Oh…nice double standard." Nickie waited for her older sister to look up at her so she could wink at Laura.

"Yeah, okay. I still don't know what it does."

"Wait, lemme see." Emily stood beside Nickie, peered down at the second orb, and pressed the small round button. The little door at the bottom opened like the other one did, letting out that tiny, glowing strand of iron. "See?"

"Hey, maybe your ring's magic is making broken things work again," Nickie said. "Actually, that *kind* of makes sense."

"Except for the first time the ring did something weird on its own—just a blast of air when Speed stank up my room."

Nickie shrugged. "Maybe it thought our dog was broken. I think Chuck's said the exact same thing once or —ah!" She jerked her hand away from the silver-glowing string, and the iron orb toppled onto the table with a *thunk*.

"What was that?"

"It *shocked* me." Nickie shook her hand out and tried to relieve the pain.

"I don't know." Emily eyed her with an unsure smile. "The other one was just fine. Let me see." She set her orb on the table and turned Nickie's hand over. "Oh. Ouch."

"Told you." Nickie frowned at the purple streaks across the pads of her thumb and index finger. "That flipping hurts."

"It actually shocked you?" Laura set down the dagger and walked around the table to see for herself. "Whoa."

Nickie prodded the marks with her other finger and winced. "That's not good. Can't hold a pick if two of the fingers I need feel like they're on fire."

Emily reached toward the shorter iron thread protruding from the second orb. No one stopped her from poking at it, but nothing happened, either. "Huh. So I'm immune to electric iron string? Laura, you give it a try." She grabbed the orb and held it out toward her sister.

"Uh, no thanks. I like my fingers the way they are."

"Yeah, I get that." Emily touched the dangling thread again, then pulled it out as far as she could stretch her arms. "Weird."

"Hey, be careful with that." Nickie backed away. "I'm gonna go put some ice on this." She headed into the kitchen.

"You know, despite the fact that I'm still not gonna test this theory myself, I think it's safe to assume that maybe my ring helped me make those specifically for you." Laura folded her arms and nodded at the iron spheres.

"You mean, like, I'm the *only* one who can touch these things?"

"Em, look at your hand."

Emily glanced down to see the copper ring on her thumb pulsing with a soft orange light. She dropped the string, and the light faded. "That's cool and everything." When she touched the string again, the light on her ring returned. "But I don't think an iron yo-yo's gonna do much to a Gorafrex."

"Well, if it's shocking or burning everyone else, you're still the only person who can figure it out." Laura shrugged and eyed the length of glowing iron string Emily spread out on the table. "Do they go back in?"

Which was what they did when Emily pressed the tiny

round button on each orb. "Like a retractable tape measure. Just apparently not as useful."

The sound of ice clattering into the sink came from the kitchen, followed by Nickie shouting, "What the—" Whatever word she said next was muffled, and Laura and Emily exchanged a worried glance before rushing into the kitchen.

"Nickie?"

"Are you—holy what?"

A small purple bubble floated just in front of Nickie's face as she turned toward them, then it drifted down onto her hand stretched over the sink. When it landed on her burned fingers, it settled into the wounds and disappeared beneath her skin. "Guess I don't need a wand for healing anymore."

Nickie gestured at her hand over the sink, and with a flash of her ring, another healing purple bubble formed at her fingertips and headed for the burns. That was the last one, the marks on her thumb and index finger were gone.

"Is that what the rings are for?" Laura asked, drawing hers and frowning at it. "To replace our wands?"

Emily cocked her head. "Aw. I like my wand."

"Well, yeah. But maybe we don't need them." Laura set hers on the kitchen counter, then stepped back and scanned the kitchen. She focused on the bunch of bananas in a bowl beside the fridge. She reached out toward them, her silver ring flashed, and a banana snapped from the bunch and drifted across the room into her hand. Grinning, she pointed the fruit at Emily. "This was exactly what I meant to do. No wand. No spellcasting; at least, not the way we're used to doing it."

"Huh." Emily eyed the banana with a raised eyebrow, then pointed at it. Her copper ring flashed, the banana peel split open in Laura's hand, and yellow-white goo fell from her hand onto the floor.

"Ew." Laura stepped away from the splattered mess, then sighed when she realized her hand hadn't escaped the banana gloop. "Em, I realize you're just trying to be funny—"

"Taste it." Emily's eyes were wide with excitement above a tiny smirk.

"What?" Her oldest sister eyed her warily. "I'm not gonna taste your squashed banana."

"Do it."

"No. I'm gonna clean up this mess. Better yet, why don't *you* clean it up—hey."

"Oh, fine. I'll taste it." Nickie reached out and swiped her finger along Laura's hand before sticking it and the gelatinous goo into her mouth. She laughed. "Oh, my god."

"Right?" Emily grinned and nodded.

"Laura, you have to taste it," Nickie pushed Laura's own hand toward her.

"Ugh, you two." Laura licked the back of her hand, the empty banana peel dangling in her fingers. "There. I tasted it. So now let's cut it with the—" She smacked her lips, recognizing the taste. "Is that..."

"Banana *pudding*." Emily looked like a madwoman about to enact her master plan for world domination. "Without any other ingredients. Or a wand."

Laura licked the back of her hand again, then tossed the banana peel in the trash beside the fridge. "Okay. Are we agreed the no-wands theory is a go?"

"I'm gonna agree with you one hundred percent on that," Nickie said, tearing off a paper towel from the roll.

"I got it." Emily took the paper towel from her sister and squatted to wipe up the banana pudding she'd made with the ring's help. She glanced up at her sisters. "This makes a lot more sense now, doesn't it?"

"What's that?" Laura cocked her head, smiling.

"The rings make the best of our magic stronger. Focused. They take what we're really good at doing and make it better."

"Right." Laura squinted in thought as Emily finished cleaning up and tossed the paper towel. "Nickie's is pretty obvious."

"My music."

"Isn't it always?" Emily laughed.

"Mine…" Laura frowned.

"Artifacts," Nickie said. "Objects. Finding them, making them, using them. That's always been your thing."

Laura grinned. "True. And Emily?"

"Makes a mean banana pudding." Nickie laughed.

"Why, thank you." Emily stepped back and gave her sisters a low, dramatic bow. When neither of them continued the revelation of her personal specialty with magic, she folded her arms and smirked at them. "I'm just really good at creating something better than what's already there."

"There it is." Laura grinned at her sisters. "You know, Em, it'd be super great if you could create us a way to track down the Gorafrex before it starts wreaking human havoc all over Austin."

Emily snorted. "Oh, yeah. Sure. I'll get right on that."

CHAPTER TWENTY-FIVE

The Gorafrex reached into its host's mind to be sure the house in front of it was the right place. Even in the middle of the night, the purple front door was unmistakable, as were the numbers nailed to the exterior wall beside it. The Gorafrex moved inside the woman's body toward the door. The woman, however, was missing some sort of key to enter her quarters. Hardly an obstacle. With a flick of its host's wrist, the Gorafrex summoned a large crimson bubble with streaks of crackling red energy around it and sent it at the purple door.

The wood split on contact, exploding backward into the human's house in a burst of sawdust and wood fragments. The Gorafrex snapped its fingers, and all the lights within clicked on at once.

"This is what they've become?" the woman muttered in a voice that wasn't completely her own. She brushed her fingers over the back of the brown leather couch in the living room, then glanced at the splintered debris on the floor. "After all this time, they've forgotten what they are.

Why they're here. And they've forgotten about me." The woman's face twisted into a vengeful sneer.

She stepped into the living room and turned in a slow circle, taking in the pictures on the mantle of a woman standing alone with mountains in the background, a river, the beach, tall white buildings. "Pathetic."

Another blood-red bubble crackling with fiery energy rose in her palm, and she threw it toward the center of the room. The low coffee table and the loveseat flew backward to crash into the far wall, and the rug beneath let off a thin curl of acrid smoke from singed fibers.

The Gorafrex moved its host into the center of the room and sat cross-legged on the rug. "They will come."

A soft mewl rose from behind her, and she glanced sideways at the floor to see a small, lithe gray cat padding curiously toward her. "At least I found something useful in this waste." She held out her hand, and the cat rubbed its face against her fingers before climbing up into the woman's lap. It sat there, purring beneath what felt like its owner's calming affection.

"They will come," the Gorafrex repeated. It stopped stroking the cat and instead took a firm grip upon the back of the animal's neck. "Then I will take from them what I need and finish what I started."

The house pet let out a strangled croak, and the woman squeezed even tighter.

CHAPTER TWENTY-SIX

Emily showed up to work the next morning feeling like a million bucks. "A wand instead of a ring." She chuckled and finished mincing the garlic for the soup Chef Ansler had added to the menu. "Sure, I sewed all those pockets for a wand..." She shrugged. "Fair trade for a super-boost of my strongest magic."

"Hadstrom!"

"Yes, Chef."

"Five minutes, and we need to move on to the wild mushroom."

"Yes, Chef."

She didn't look up from her workstation in the bustling kitchen, moving as quickly as her fingers and her knife would allow. "I've already got soups down," she muttered, sliding the garlic off the cutting board and into a large stainless-steel pot. "Obviously. But they're gonna keep me here as long as they had me on vegetables. Or longer." She grabbed the lemon in front of her, quartered it, measured out the juice. "I need to blow him away with something incredible if I want to move up. Can't do that if he's already got the menu down…"

She stopped cutting and glanced at her hand wrapped around the handle of her Shun chef's knife. The copper ring on her thumb glinted at her as if it had winked. Lifting her head, she glanced around the bustling kitchen at every head chef and assisting chef, all of them focused on their work, completing their part of Chef Ansler's vision of a menu. "I can do so much better than this. Screw the rules."

Everything she needed was right in front of her. Her magic through her ring could take care of the rest. "Today, I'm going all out."

She tapped her workstation and nodded at the prepped vegetables beside the pot. Her ring flashed, the produce disappeared, and a muffled *plop* rose from the pot of soup. Stifling back her enthusiasm, she pointed to each ingredient in turn; every item minced, diced, pared, sliced, and shaved itself into the pot the way she wanted. In less than a minute, she'd completed what would have normally taken her five minutes.

Emily bit her lip and eyed the pot again. "Just make it good." She tapped the edge of the pot, her ring flashed, and she grinned.

The flame still flickered beneath the burner, and she stirred her creation a few times.

"Three minutes," her advising Potager Chef called.

"Finished," Emily told him. "Moving on. Wild mushroom."

"Really?" Anthony stepped toward her station with a suspicious frown.

With a nod, Emily turned from her station to grab the

tray of ingredients she'd set aside for the second soup option. She snuck a glance at her supervisor at the potager station, who'd brought a tasting spoon of her first soup to his lips. He blinked, and when Emily set down her tray, Anthony stormed off across the kitchen with a side dish of her soup. She bit back a smile and got to work on the wild mushroom soup.

Two minutes later, Chef Ansler stood behind her, watching. Emily didn't look up, and of course she couldn't use her magic now. "Hadstrom, what did you do to the garbanzo-leek?"

"I made it exactly the way you wanted, Chef." She fought to keep her voice even and her face expressionless as she cut the wild mushrooms into thin strips. From the corner of her eye, she saw him take another bite from the side dish.

"Hmm. You didn't add anything? Change it in any way?"

Just a little magic. No big deal. "No, Chef."

For a few seconds, he stood there, then he leaned toward her and whispered, "You've got my attention, Emily. Do something important with it."

He clapped his hands and rushed away. "Change of plans. We do things a certain way in this kitchen, but today, we're going to break the rules. I want every station to go taste the garbanzo-leek. I want this week's menu paired to what you pick up in there. If you can add a dish to it, excellent. If not, scrap it and start over. We're gonna blow this outta the park." Then he left the kitchen for reasons only Chef Ansler knew as the chefs swarmed Emily's station.

She ignored them and kept working on the wild mushrooms as one after another of her superior chefs at Meadowlark Tavern dipped their spoons into the stainless-steel pot on the burner and learned what they could from what the junior chef had done.

Creating from what's already there. She forced back a smirk and glanced at the copper ring again. *Let's do this.*

Nickie pulled her guitar case out of the backseat of Laura's car and closed the door. She peered through the open passenger side door and smiled. "Thanks for dropping me off."

"No problem. It's good to have your own car again."

"Yup." Nickie lifted her keys and dangled them by her face. "Time to get going."

"Where's Chuck?"

"Oh, he's got meetings all day. I'll probably see him tonight."

"You have a show, right?"

"Yup. At Tina's."

Laura squinted. "The laundromat."

"That's the one. Before you ask again, I'm doing it 'cause it's fun. And she's a friend."

Her sister shrugged behind the wheel. "Sounds like good reasons to me."

"What are you up to?"

"I'm gonna see if I can find anything else on the Gorafrex. Maybe there's some kinda history book, some account of what happened *before* everyone got on this ship."

Nickie widened her eyes. "You think something survived from that long ago?"

"Maybe. I have a few ideas of where to start."

"Good luck."

"Thanks. See ya."

Nickie closed the car door and watched her sister drive away before she went to her black Camry and stuck her guitar case on the passenger seat. Then she headed out of Chuck's neighborhood.

She parked relatively close to Shoal Beach, just east of where Barton Creek intersected the Colorado River. Her Dad used to tell her when she was a kid, "There's no better place to practice than in public. Most people pretend they don't hear, and you get to pretend you don't care."

A little sliver of sandy grass ran along the river right off the bike trail. It was as secluded and unoccupied today as Nickie always found it. She settled in the grass, a thick cluster of trees at her back and listened to the sounds of the city and the occasional whir of rubber bike tires passing behind her.

With a sigh, she gazed across the river and enjoyed the cool shade. Then, she opened her guitar case, lifted her guitar into her lap, and tuned the strings. "Just a little break," she reminded herself. "Then I can help Laura look for information."

Nickie closed her eyes and didn't take out her pick this time. Just a little gentle strumming on the strings, and she let her fingers take over. The wind rustled through the leaves around her, casting flickering shadows and lifting her hair away from her face. She played, and a small pressure built behind her temple.

The drumming started in her head. Her fingers slipped off the strings, and she took a sharp breath. "Again? I thought I figured this out." Nickie gritted her teeth and recalled her discovery yesterday. She ignored the pain and the deafening volume of the Gorafrex's chaotic rhythm— did her best, at least— and her fingers formed the chords to the song her Dad had sung all her life.

The branches shook overhead, rustling violently. Nickie hummed the lullaby proven to make the pounding in her head stop, then something thumped onto the ground beside her. She opened her eyes and felt a warm, gentle hand on her shoulder. She paused playing as a Tree Folk crouched beside her, golden whiskers fluttering around his face. He pressed a finger to his lips, and his brow furrowed in a dark frown.

"Uh, hi," Nickie whispered, staring at him.

"We heard your song." The elf spoke in a low voice and glanced around at the trees between where they sat and the bike path on the other side. "We shouldn't have."

"My—how'd you get here?"

The elf smirked. "We are the Tree Folk. Not the Boggy Creek Folk."

"So you…live in all the trees?"

"We are with them, more or less, whenever we wish to be. I need you to listen, witch. If my people discover I was here to warn you, I will pay a price for it." He shrugged and grinned. "But I am a fan."

Nickie's smile was small and weak. "I appreciate that, but I'm a little confused about…did you say you're here to warn me?"

The tree elf nodded and glanced across the river. "The

music you were just playing, we've heard it before."

"It's part of what helped my ancestors seal the Gorafrex in the prison they—"

"No." The elf shook his head and stared at her with his piercing blue gaze. "*That* song is the echo of the Gorafrex's call. They are like magnetic forces. Do you understand?"

"Can you explain it more than that?" Nickie peeped behind her through the trees at two pairs of jogging shoes slapping over the concrete sidewalk until they disappeared down the path.

This is definitely the weirdest place to have the weirdest conversation.

Those ice-blue eyes blinked at her, and the elf's face softened. "Play that song, and you call the Gorafrex to you."

The drums began building in Nickie's head again, and she clenched her eyes shut. "I have to play it," she muttered. "That's the only way to…" She rubbed her forehead. "I'm hearing that thing's drums in my head."

"The Gorafrex is calling to you. To all of your kind. This is how it will find you. Like nectar draws honeybees, yes?"

"I'm pretty sure nectar doesn't want to kill the bees."

The elf dipped his head with a slow smile. "The fact remains; the Gorafrex seeks all witches and wizards, as its kind has always done. It will find you faster than any others of your race if you play that song without your kin."

"My sisters?"

"There is a piece—" The elf cocked his head and clenched his eyes. "I must go."

"What? Wait. A piece of what?"

"Do not summon the Gorafrex on your own. Your magic is strong, but it is not enough."

"What were you going to say?"

The elf scrambled across the grass and leapt into the closest tree. The branches rocked violently again, knocking a few green leaves loose to flutter to the ground. The pounding drums flared in Nickie's head, bringing her to the verge of a full-blown headache. Her hands shook as she returned her guitar to its case, closed the latches, and put her hands in her lap to still them.

If I can't play the song, how am I supposed to get this to stop?

CHAPTER TWENTY-SEVEN

Laura stood in the foyer, waiting for the house to finish turning and folding. "Where is he?" she muttered.

When everything stopped moving, she faced the same door with the tiny square mirror in its center. "Again? Really? That's a little vain, Gilroy, even for you." She stepped forward and opened the door to the mirror room, finding it the same as yesterday, except Gilroy and his pedestal weren't in the far corner.

She squinted. "What are you up to?"

"And you call yourself a scientist. Ha!"

Laura started, and Gilroy spit out a wheezing laugh, his stone eyes bulging in his stone face. He'd moved his pedestal directly in front of another mirror just inside the door.

"For the millionth time, I'm an archaeologist."

"I know what you are," he whispered.

"Then act like it. I have a few more questions for you."

"Doesn't everyone?"

She frowned at the bust. "How do we find the Gorafrex?"

"No one finds the Gorafrex, ya big dummy. *It* finds *you*. And all the others, if it gets what it wants."

"What does it want?"

"To find you and all the others." The smug statue would've folded his arms if he'd had any.

"Yeah, very helpful. Is there a way for us to track it before it takes over another human?"

"Does nectar track honeybees—huh." He scrunched up his face and rolled his eyes toward the ceiling. "I feel like that's already been said before…"

"Okay, listen up, Gilroy. I need you to tell me where that Gorafrex is so we can put it back in that prison before things get worse. Even one possessed human is one too many; now, there are two. If this thing keeps running around hopping in and out of people, we're gonna have a whole bunch of inexperienced Peabrains using their magic with as much control as a toddler driving a semi. Help me out here."

The bust blinked at her, his stony face expressionless.

"Right. Not a question." Laura let out a huge sigh and rolled her shoulders. "Where is the Gorafrex right now?"

"Within a human host. Obviously."

Laura folded her arms and glared at him. "Do you really know everything?"

"No."

She froze. "Wait, what?"

"Are you deaf? I said no."

"Oh, that…changes everything I thought I knew about you."

Gilroy shrugged.

"Okay, there's gotta be a better way to phrase this. Hold on. Is there anyone else who knows how we can pinpoint the Gorafrex's location short of walking aimlessly around Austin and hoping we bump into it?"

"Yes."

"Huh. Now we're getting somewhere. Who is it?"

"Define *it*." Gilroy wiggled his eyebrows.

"You know, I'm *this* close from shoving over that pedestal and leaving you in a few pieces on the floor." Laura took a deep breath. "Starting over. What's the name of the person who knows how to pinpoint the Gorafrex's location without randomly crossing its path?"

"*The* person? There's more than one, you know."

"Oh. My. God. Do I really have to ask that all over again with one little change?"

"Do you really have to ask that question?"

Trying not to explode and knock the know-it-all bust to the floor, Laura tried again. "What's the name of the person most likely to help us pinpoint the Gorafrex's location in a specific way rather than just hoping we find it again in the city?"

"Nickie Hadstrom."

"*What?*"

The mirror room bursted with light, the glow from every reflective surface building upon itself until it was blinding. Laura shielded her eyes.

"Laura?" An almost-deafening voice echoed a thousand times from within a thousand mirrors.

"Nickie?" Laura gazed up at her sister's face; everywhere she looked, her sister's face had appeared with a backdrop of leafy branches rustling in a small breeze. "What's wrong? Did something happen?"

"Yes and no." Nickie squeezed her eyes shut and grimaced. "The drums are back."

Laura's head felt like it was going to burst with the volume of her sister's voice in sudden surround-sound. "Okay. So, play the lullaby."

"I can't." Nickie sucked in a breath and groaned. "The… the Tree Folk told me what it's for. It's…can you come get me? I'm sorry. It's this headache." She blinked her eyes open, and they looked unfocused and hazy.

"Yeah, okay. Hey, it's faster if you go to the Clubhouse. You have your keyring with you?"

"Mm-hmm."

"Okay. Go now. I'll be right there." The mirrors flashed all at once, rippling a few seconds until they fell perfectly still, and the light faded. Nickie's face was gone.

Laura turned toward Gilroy and scowled. "How long have you known Nickie had the answer to my question?"

"About ten minutes."

"How long has she known the answer to my question?"

"About ten minutes."

Laura puffed out a breath. "Lotta help you are."

She turned and opened the door to the mirror room and stepped into the foyer. The house rumbled and turned around her, shifting to its original size and shape. The minute the dining room became the dining room, Laura rushed straight to the table, and all the iron weapons on it, and snatched her keys from her purse. Then she pressed her thumb to the coin-shaped keyring with her thumbprint etched into it and disappeared.

She blinked into existence in the middle of the Clubhouse's single room. "Nickie?"

"Hey." Her sister lay on her back on the cherry-red futon, one arm thrown over her eyes.

"Are you okay?" Laura knelt beside her.

"Yeah. Good idea to come here, by the way." Nickie didn't remove her arm, but she sounded a lot less in pain. "The drums are gone. Headache's still there, though."

"Want me to get you something? I'll even go with modern medicine and grab you some aspirin."

"No, I'm good. It's getting better."

"Okay." Laura sat back on her heels. "If you're sure you're okay, I've got a few questions…"

"I figured you would."

"You went to go see the Tree Folk?"

Nickie chuckled. "I went to Shoal Beach to play a little music and get my head straight before going to Tina's. One of them found *me*."

"How?"

"Through the trees, maybe. And my music. He said they heard me play the song and that he wasn't supposed to come and warn me, but he did anyway."

"Guess we'll have to thank him for that."

Nickie slowly removed her arm from over her eyes. She appeared pale and exhausted. Blinking, she rolled her head to the side to meet her sister's gaze. "He told me I can't play that song unless I'm with 'my kin'. Which I'm hoping is you and Emily. Otherwise, I have no idea how to take that advice."

"Did he tell you why?"

"He said Dad's lullaby and the Gorafrex's drumbeat attract each other. Like magnets."

"I don't get it."

Nickie licked her lips. "You get it, Laura. Dad's lullaby calls the Gorafrex, tells it where I am, I think. And the drums are its way of luring witches and wizards to it. Because it wants us for something."

"Yeah, to kill us. That's what they do, right?"

"There's gotta be a reason for that, though. Nothing just kills other beings for the hell of it."

"Well, if there even *is* a reason, finding out what that is might help us in some way."

"Yep." Nickie pushed up to sit against the back cushion, holding out a hand when Laura reached to help. "I'm okay. Really. Sorry if I freaked you out. The elf just scampered away without really explaining much, and I didn't know what to do. Left my phone in the car, so Sister Soup in the river was my only option."

Laura let out a small laugh. "I was in the mirror room when you did that."

"Really?"

"Yep. A thousand Nickies all talking at the same time. Right after Gilroy told me you were the one person most likely to find the Gorafrex." Laura climbed onto the futon beside her sister. "That was weird timing, but it makes sense now. I was asking how we *find* it. Turns out we can't. But you can summon it."

"Summon might be a strong word."

"Well, it's close enough."

Nickie tipped her head back against the red cushion. "I think that was my first real migraine."

Laura bit her lip and studied her sister's profile. "I'm so sorry, Nickie. This whole thing wouldn't have happened if I wasn't so set on slipping through those wards in the creek and snooping around."

"Don't start beating yourself up *now*. You had no idea what those wards were protecting. Plus, that's kinda what you do, right? When you find a locked door, you either beat it down or make yourself a key."

Laura let out a wry laugh, then shook her head. "Next time I find one of these *locked doors*, I'm gonna tell you and Emily about it first. And I'll try to listen to you next time."

Nickie grinned. "Sounds like a plan."

"So, you can only play Dad's song when we're all together, ready to go up against this rogue witch-killer?"

"Yup."

"That seems like a lot of migraines in your future."

Nickie nodded, then paused. "Maybe not. They stopped the minute I came here. That's gotta mean something."

"I mean, we *did* build the Clubhouse specifically tailored to the three of us. Fingerprints and everything. We couldn't bring anyone else in here even if we wanted to."

"Maybe *that's* it. It keeps the Gorafrex's magic out."

"Good." Laura slapped her thighs and stood. "Emily's at work still, but when she's off, we should grab our weapons and get down to the Greenbelt. You can play Dad's song, that thing will show up, and we'll put it back. Until then, stay here."

"What? No way."

"Nickie, that thing's trying to draw witches and wizards to it, and it's not gonna give up. You don't hear the drums here, so you won't get headaches. Staying here keeps you safe."

"I'm not just gonna hide in the Clubhouse. Besides, I have a show to play tonight."

"In a laundromat."

"It's a *show*. I'm going."

"And what happens if the drumming starts up again, huh? Can you play a show through that?"

Nickie stood. "I'll figure it out. Chuck's gonna be there, too, like he is at every show, no matter *where* I'm playing. And I can't just tell him I've got a magical creature's witch-lure stuck in my head and have to retreat to a secret room only my sisters and I can access through our matching keyrings."

They stared at one another a few seconds, then Laura shook her head. "Fine. Will you at least keep your phone on you? Call me if anything weird happens?"

"Of course."

"If the drums come back, and they're too much for you to handle, get back here. At least until you feel better."

"Got it. Thanks."

"If I don't see you before your show, good luck."

Nickie laughed. "Well, thanks."

Laura fingered the keyring on her keys, slipped her thumb onto the coin, and popped back into their dining room.

CHAPTER TWENTY-EIGHT

"Hadstrom. Take your break. We got this." For the first time since she'd started working, the Potager Chef smiled at her and nodded.

"Um...yeah. Okay." She turned from her station and walked toward the staff room just off the kitchen. "I didn't ask for a break..."

The kitchen filled with its usual ordered chaos, though instead of the normal shouts of, "Yes, Chef," and "On it, Chef," the voices of her coworkers rose with something entirely different.

"This is the best ever."

"No one's ever done this before. It's perfect!"

"Ha! Who says we can't pair them together? A bunch of old-fashioned stiffs, if you ask me."

Emily frowned at the sight of all these people doing what they did best and yet not quite following the detailed precision Chef Ansler always upheld in his kitchen. "This looks familiar," she muttered. Instead of going into the staff room, Emily skirted around the workstations toward the swinging door from the kitchen into the restaurant's main dining room. She peered through the circular window, and her jaw dropped.

The tables were all full, as they usually were on Sundays, but the calm, poised, sophisticated air of Meadowlark Tavern didn't exist. The place was a madhouse.

Her gaze fell on one woman standing on her chair, dancing with a glass of chardonnay in hand. "I *got* this!" she shouted, then stepped her stilettos up onto the table and started dancing—to no music—with a little *whoop*.

A server rushed to the woman to quietly coax her down from the table while the rest of her party stared and laughed.

"Ma'am, please get down from the table."

"*Make* me."

A man in a business suit passed right in front of the kitchen door, yelling into his cell phone. "I don't *care* if that's not how it's done, Gary. That's how *I'm* doing it. Screw the rules. And if you don't get this done, screw you too!"

Another elderly couple at the far end of the restaurant stood together with their arms wrapped around each other, belting out a song at the tops of their lungs, oblivious that they sounded atrocious.

The server who'd failed at removing the woman from the table caught Emily's eye. He hurried toward her, and Emily stepped back so he could push open the door. "I have no idea what to do right now," he said, lowering his voice but having to be a little loud over the din. "I told Chef Ansler, and he said to let them have fun because it didn't matter. But…" He glanced back at the craziness. "How does this *not* matter. I feel like we should call the cops or something. Oh, god. They're probably not gonna tip, either."

Emily grabbed the server's arm—his name was John, she thought—and smiled. "They definitely won't tip you if you call the cops on them. Just, uh...let me try something, okay? Hospitality 101. Sit tight, and if this doesn't work, maybe we'll call a riot team, huh?"

"Oh, *god.*"

"I'm kidding. Totally kidding. Just sit tight and keep filling up their waters." She let go of his arm and turned back toward the kitchen, then paused. "Hey, you didn't eat any of the soup tonight, did you?"

"What? No."

"Good. Don't." The kitchen door shut behind her, and she hurried back to her station. "Definitely familiar," she muttered. "Definitely on a much larger scale this time. I *might* have taken it a little too far." The overblown confidence with which she'd made her magical soup had manifested in everyone else who'd eaten it—the kitchen staff *and* the patrons. "I can fix this. Just focus."

Emily pulled out the container of the wild mushroom soup she'd made at the start of her shift, which she'd been told to put away in lieu of how incredible the first one was. "Yes, Chef," she muttered, "I believe that extra ingredient you're tasting is my magic on overload."

She poured the soup into another large pot and clicked on the burner to start warming it up. Then she found a block of Gruyère cheese and shaved it into the soup, talking herself through the process. "Calmly. Realizing my mistake. That I'd been a little too full of myself. Well, at least that's actually how I'm feeling right now. And that I want to just forget this whole thing ever happened and move on with the night." She swallowed. "I really hope the servers get their tips…"

The activity in the kitchen died down a little, most of the chefs stepping away from their stations to talk to each other about how talented they were and that the dishes can make themselves for all they cared.

Emily shook her head, finished stirring the cheese into the soup, and wondered if any of them noticed her blushing. "Probably not." She dished out a little soup into as many ramekins and soup cups as she could find, snatched up a tin of clean spoons, and carried the tray of soup out of the kitchen.

The server she thought was John rushed toward her with wide eyes, biting his nails. "*This* is your great idea? Give them *more* food?"

"Trust me. This'll help." Emily nodded. "Just pass one out to everybody, okay?"

"And tell them *what*?"

"That it's on the house. That we're sampling a new menu item, and they came in on a special night, so they get to try it. I dunno. Tell them whatever you want, but make sure everybody tastes it, okay? How many people are in the dining room right now?"

The server glanced over his shoulder, his lips moving in silent calculation. "Fifty-two."

"Wow. Okay. I'm gonna go dish up some more and bring you another tray. Have the other servers help. Things will go back to normal soon."

"How could you *possibly* know that?"

"I just do. Go on." She handed over the tray, then turned

to repeat the process all over again. Dishing soup. Traying cups and bowls. Back and forth until she had to wipe the sweat from her forehead with the sleeve of her chef's coat. "Okay. First glimpse of what it's like to be in charge of everything. At least when I run my own kitchen, I'll have had experience doing basically everything." That made her laugh a little. "It's really not funny."

Finally, the head server popped into the kitchen to tell her everyone had received their samples and seemed to be enjoying them. The woman glanced at all the chefs, who were at this point making themselves dinner, unaware of what was happening in the dining room. Her eyes grew wide, then she spun and swiftly left.

"Almost done," Emily muttered. She dished out fourteen more samples of wild mushroom and humility soup, then made her rounds through the kitchen. Her coworkers seemed more than happy to receive someone else's cooking, and she found herself repeating over and over, "I just wanted to show my appreciation for what you do." That was a tough enough pill to swallow, though it was true. The skilled and experienced chefs at Meadowlark Tavern seemed pleased enough to give her concoction a try.

Slowly, one by one, the chefs stopped what they were doing, blinked around the kitchen, and avoided each other's gazes. Thankfully, they'd gone through all the orders on the line with a full dining room, so they at least hadn't made any of their customers *wait* for their ego-inflating dinner. Apparently, Emily's magic had been strong enough to feed them exactly what she was feeling—again, but this time with the intention to set things back on track.

"Oh, man." With a huge sigh, Emily leaned against the outside of the walk-in fridge and closed her eyes. "I'm so glad that worked."

"Hadstrom."

She jumped to attention. "Yes, Chef."

Anthony approached her and cleared his throat. His neck was a little red under his chef's collar, and he didn't exactly look at her. "Break's over. We filled up tonight, so there aren't any more tables coming in. Just focus on cleaning up. Clear your station. Then you can head out."

"Yes, Chef."

He cleared his throat again and nodded at the walk-in behind her. "Right. Good work tonight."

"Thank you, Chef." Only when he walked away did she let herself smile.

When she finished cleaning her station, washing a few dishes, and prepping for her next shift tomorrow, she went to the staff room to grab her purse from her locker. The server whose name was John—as it was written on the tape on the locker he rummaged through—stopped when he saw her and smiled. "I don't know how in any alternate universe tonight could ever be possible, but whatever you did worked."

Emily laughed. "Good."

"Yeah. Everyone settled down after that. I think the old singing couple were just really drunk at the end."

"Did the tips work out for you?"

"*Oh*, yeah." John shut his locker and leaned toward her, though there was no one else in the staff room to hear him.

"I still have a few tables left, but so far, I haven't made less than forty-percent. I'd do this every night to keep that up."

Emily burst out laughing, which brought a confused smile to John's face. "I wouldn't. No tips in it for me."

"Fair enough. Hey, you done for the night?"

"Yeah. Chef-in-training, right? I get sent home early. See you tomorrow?"

"Yeah. I'm stepping outside for a break." He nodded toward the kitchen's back door on the other side of the staff room. "Come on." With a grin, John headed out first. Shaking her head, Emily followed, ready to be done with the night and start over tomorrow.

The minute the back door closed behind them, John pulled a pack of cigarettes from his back pocket and held them toward her. "Want one?"

"Oh. No thanks."

He stuck one in his mouth and lit it, the flame lighting up his face in the parking lot beneath the streetlamps. "I'm serious. That was the craziest night I've ever seen in food and bev. Maybe even worse than catering."

Emily stepped away from the smoke as politely as she could.

"Oh. Sorry." John watched his cigarette smoke for a minute, then stepped downwind of her and offered a sheepish smile. "Bad habit, I know. I shouldn't have started it the first place. Waiting tables makes it hard to quit."

"Hey, it's all good."

"So, chef-in-training. I don't think we've officially met."

"Emily."

"John." They shook, and he smiled through another

drag of his cigarette. "Now I know who to go to with our rowdy customers."

She laughed. "I was just fixing my own—"

He squinted at her. "Your own..."

"Nothing. It's stupid."

"What, you slipped up with an order and tried to make up for it?"

"Something like that."

John exhaled a cloud of smoke into the night sky and shrugged. "Waiting tables has its challenges, right? I enjoy it. I don't think I could handle working in a high-end kitchen like you do."

"Oh, because we all get yelled at and belittled and pressured to make the dish right or not at all?"

He chuckled. "Yeah."

Emily raised an eyebrow. "I think somebody's watching too many reality cooking shows."

"Oh, it's not like that?"

"Sometimes." They both laughed. "Mostly it just takes a lot of focus. And, yeah, being able to take criticism from people who know more than you and have way more experience has its challenges, I guess."

"Like tonight."

She grinned and nodded. "Yeah. Like tonight."

"And you like cooking?"

"Wouldn't be here if I didn't."

John lifted his cigarette toward his lips, but paused. "That's good to hear. Not enough people do what they do because they want to instead of because they think they have to."

"Well, I guess I just know what I want."

He smirked. "I can see that."

I actually might be starting to like this guy if he wasn't a smoker. Bummer.

"So..." she pointed her keys toward her Honda and leaned in that direction. "I'm calling it a night."

"Okay. Hey, what time do you get off tomorrow?"

"Well, that depends on—" Emily stopped and cocked her head. The urgent, energetic cadence of a drumbeat echoed from really far away. "Do you hear that?"

"Um...what am I listening for?"

He can't hear it. Great. "Nothing. Sorry. Hey, I gotta go. Nice to meet you officially." She tried not to run from her car.

"Everything okay?" John called after her with a hesitant smile.

"Yep. Have a good night."

"Yeah, you—"

She'd already slipped into her car and shut the door before he could finish. She pulled out of the parking lot behind Meadowlark Tavern, tires squealing. "Gorafrex's on the loose again. Because humans can't hear it. And I definitely heard those drums. So..." Forcing herself to take a breath, she reached for her purse and stopped. Then she waited to take out her phone until she'd pulled over at the next gas station. "Time to be smarter about this."

Laura answered on the second ring. "Hey."

"I heard it. The drums. I heard the drums."

"Whoa, Em. Slow down. Are you okay?"

"Yeah, I'm fine. Just had a really weird night, and this isn't exactly helping."

"Okay. Where are you?"

"A gas station by Meadowlark. I'm okay. I just heard the drums."

"Did your ring do anything weird?" Laura asked. "Like buzzing or—"

"Nope. But I thought I should give you a call. Maybe now's a good time to get together and try grabbing this thing before it slips into any more humans. Or something worse."

"Yeah, we should do that."

"Okay. Want me to call Nickie?"

"She probably won't answer. She's got a show—" There was a long silence on the other end of the phone.

"Laura?"

"What street is Tina's laundromat on?"

"Uh…off Lavaca. I'm not sure what street, but it's close —oh. Crap."

"We need to get over there. Nickie has no idea."

Emily threw her car into drive and said, "I'll see you there." Then she ended the call, tossed her phone onto the passenger seat, and drove toward the laundromat like a woman who needed a fajita.

CHAPTER TWENTY-NINE

Chuck held Nickie by the shoulders and studied her with a small frown. "You okay, babe? You look a little off."

"I'm fine. Just a little tired. I think I had a migraine earlier."

"Ouch. You take anything for it?"

"No." She wrapped her arms around his waist and smiled up at him. "It's gone now. Right in time for me to play."

"Hmm." He bent down to kiss her, then pulled back just a little to look her in the eyes. "I can't wait."

Nickie laughed and bent to pick up her dark-blue Strat. She slipped the strap over her head and shoulder. "I love that you still get excited about laundromat gigs."

"Are you kidding? I get excited when you play in an empty room." He glanced past all the washing machines and dryers of Soapy Days Twenty-Four-Hour Laundromat and gave her a wide grin. "Which this obviously isn't. I'm pretty sure I'm your biggest fan."

She pulled him in for another kiss. "Let's keep it that way." She winked at him, then headed toward the tiny box stage beside Tina's small office. About a dozen chairs had been set up between the stage and the first row of dryers, all the laundry-folding tables moved to the back. Every chair had someone in it, and more people mingled behind the first row of dryers and waited for Nickie.

Nickie smiled and gave a few 'heys' to familiar faces, then stepped onto the tiny stage. A furious round of clapping and 'whoop-whoops' went up. She gazed over at her friend Tina Lennick standing behind the dryers, grinning from ear to ear under her short, pink-dyed hair. Nickie nodded at her as the rest of the small crowd applauded.

Chuck stuck his fingers in his mouth and whistled.

Nickie made sure her portable amp and microphone were on, then she grabbed the XLR cable, plugged it into her Strat, and stepped up to the mic.

"Can everybody hear me okay?"

The applause and cheers grew louder with several 'yeahs.'

She smirked. "Excellent. Wow, look at this, huh? Big crowd for a laundromat on a Monday night." People shouted and whooped. "Thanks, Tina, for having me here. And thank *you*, everybody, for coming out tonight. Hey, and if you're here just to do your laundry, at least you have some music to chill to, right?" She pointed to the woman at the far end of the room, who stopped shoving dirty clothes into a washing machine to wave and give a whoop of excitement.

"Yeah..." Nickie chuckled. "You know, this was one of the first places I ever played when I started doing this regularly. I love being back here, so I won't make you wait any longer. I'm Nickie Hadstrom. This first song is called 'String in a Bottle.'"

She stepped back to pull her lime-green pick from the front pocket of her black skinny jeans, raised her eyebrows at Chuck, and strummed the first chord. It filled the laundromat, and she shot an open-mouthed grin at the tiny crowd. They all grinned.

Before she even started singing, the audience nodded to the beat of one of her newer bluesy jams. And Nickie was just getting started.

Laura wanted to speed. She zoomed with her window opened, but was forced to settle on four miles per hour over the limit. It was only a fifteen-minute drive to Soapy Days, but even that felt too long. The light ahead turned red, and she knocked her fist against the steering wheel. "There needs to be some kind of magical exemption for traffic lights." She glanced at the three iron daggers on the passenger seat. "No. It's better to be safe." She stuck the daggers in the glovebox before the light turned green. "That's a little better."

When she pulled up in front of the laundromat, she saw Emily's Honda in the long line of cars outside the strip of stores and bars. Emily stood just inside the door behind a small crowd. She spied Nickie on the tiny stage, rocking out and intermittently lifting her face to the microphone.

As Laura turned got out of her car, the silver ring on her finger buzzed. "Aw, man."

Emily turned to look through the window and saw

Laura stepping onto the sidewalk. The youngest Hadstrom sister slipped out of the laundromat, letting out a low whine from Nickie's playing before it was dampened by the door shutting.

"Hey." Emily walked toward her sister. "Your ring doing the little buzzy thing too?"

"Yep." Laura opened her passenger-side door and pulled two daggers out of the glovebox. "These are still, you know, disguised. But we should have them just in case."

Emily took the offered dagger and stared at it. "Part of me really wants to use this just to get it over with. I mean, I know it's only been two days, but it feels a lot longer."

"I know. How's she doin' in there?"

"Great. Really wowing the laundry crowd."

Laura shook her head with a small smile. "At least she's having fun."

Nickie bent over her guitar for a fast-paced solo, her long dark hair dangling over the neck of the guitar before she tossed her head back and took a few steps across the stage.

Then the drums returned.

"Please tell me *you* hear it," Emily said.

"Of course I hear it. It doesn't sound close, but we probably shouldn't take any chances."

"Chances with what?"

Laura blinked at her, then gestured toward the laundromat with her dagger. "There are a whole bunch of people in there. Humans. If this Gorafrex shows up, we can't just fight it off in front of everybody. In front of Chuck."

"Right. What do we do?"

The drums became louder, rising from two streets over now instead of three.

"First, we need to make sure Nickie's okay."

"What's wrong with her?"

"She was hearing the drums again today." Laura headed toward the door and watched her sister perform.

"That sucks. The headache came back?"

"Yeah, and I think it was worse."

"She can just play Dad's lullaby, right? Problem solved."

Laura frowned. "I forgot to tell you…"

"Tell me what?"

"One of the Tree Folk came to her, told her she can't play Dad's lullaby unless the three of us are together. Because it…*calls* the Gorafrex to her. Seems the drums are supposed to lure in any witches and wizards who hear them."

"Are you serious?" Emily sighed. "Yeah, that's your serious face. So she's gonna hear the drums. And she can't play the lullaby to get them out of her head."

"She can. Just not with so many humans around. Oh, no."

"What?" Emily joined her sister at the laundromat windows where Nickie was frowning on stage and grimacing more than grinning as she played.

"Looks like she hears 'em too." Laura opened the door to the blast of high-volume guitar. Emily followed behind, meeting Chuck's gaze and giving him a little nod. He smiled back, bobbing his head to the music, but then gave Emily a curious expression, likely from her giving off a worried vibe.

The two sisters moved behind the crowd. Laura's ring

buzzed on her thumb, but she couldn't hear the drums from inside the laundromat. *Hopefully, that means the Gorafrex hasn't gotten too close.*

Nickie sang another verse into the microphone, and as soon as she finished, she played a flourishing little riff and ended the song.

"That wasn't the last line," Emily muttered.

"Yeah, she's hurting."

The few dozen people in the laundromat burst into applause. Chuck clapped with them, but he wore a small frown as he studied his girlfriend.

"Chuck can tell something's wrong."

Laura side-eyed Chuck and nodded at Em.

"Thanks, you guys. Thank you. I'm gonna take a quick five. So, uh, wash your clothes if you need to." A few people laughed, and Nickie pulled her strap over her head and put the Strat on its stand beside the amp. She ran a hand through her hair and hurried offstage.

Laura and Emily skirted around the crowd toward her.

"Nickie."

Their sister turned, and her eyes widened when she saw Laura. "I'm hearing it again. Right now. I'm trying to play a fricking show." Her voice trembled, and she clenched her eyes shut.

"Yeah, I know." Laura grabbed her by the shoulders. "Because it's here."

"What?"

"It probably doesn't know *we're* here," Emily added. "But we heard the drumming outside. It's up to something."

"This is the worst timing ever." Nickie put a hand to her

forehead and let out a little laugh. "I have to play the lullaby, don't I?"

"Not with all these people here. We need to get them out, then you can play, and we'll be ready."

"Okay." Nickie swallowed. "I'm gonna…" She headed away from them, then turned back and blinked at her sisters as Chuck walked around a couple and came up behind her. "I'm gonna get Chuck out first," she mouthed at them.

Laura nodded. "We'll take care of everyone else."

Nickie turned away from them and toward Chuck, who gave her a frown of concern.

"Are you okay?" he asked, reaching out to tuck her hair behind her ears.

She nodded and smiled at him. "Yeah. I think that migraine's coming back."

"I'll go talk to Tina—"

"No. Don't do that." She grabbed his hands and looked up into his blue eyes, trying to ignore the pounding of the drums in her head. "I'm gonna keep going. I *do* need a really big favor from you, though."

"Sure."

"Can you go to the CVS and grab me this bottle. It's like… aspirin and acetaminophen and Benadryl all mixed together in one. That's really the only thing that's been helping. Some places don't have it, so you might have to go check out a few."

"That actually exists?"

Man, I hate having to lie to him. "Yeah. I took the last one I had earlier today. I'm gonna keep playing. I think I can hold on a little longer, but I'd really like to have those in case it gets worse."

"Yeah, whatever you need." Chuck pulled her in for a tight hug. "Must be a really bad one."

Nickie let out a wry chuckle. "Pretty much the worst."

He kissed the top of her head and pulled away. "Yeah, I'll go find that stuff for you. Aspirin, acetaminophen…"

"And Benadryl. Yeah." They nodded at each other.

"Okay. Okay. But if it gets bad, don't try to push through it, all right? I know you really enjoy playing here…" He glanced around at the inside of Soapy Days and the small crowd who'd come to watch Nickie Hadstrom on a Monday. "But it's just a laundromat. Most people don't know about it. Most people won't know if you have to pull out, okay?"

"Yeah, I know. Hopefully I won't have to."

"Okay. I'll be back as soon as I can."

"Thank you."

He kissed her again and moved through the crowd and rows of chairs toward the door.

Nickie's hand shook as she raised it to her pounding temple. When Chuck opened the door out onto the sidewalk, she heard the drums all too clearly. Her head jerked up to find her sisters, both of whom stared outside after Chuck. They looked at Nickie with grim expressions.

Nickie watched as Chuck's car pulled away from the street, and she knew he was safe for now. *Looking for a nonexistent bottle of pain-relievers will keep him away while we handle this.*

She walked toward her sisters, knowing her five-minute break was almost up. "That was fast," Emily said.

"Yeah. He'll be gone for a while. You guys figure out how to get everybody out of here without mass hysteria?"

"Not yet." Laura glanced through the windows again. The drums were louder, closer, and all three sisters expected to find themselves up against the Gorafrex any minute. "You think you could ask Tina for a favor? Get her to tell everyone there's a leak in the—"

A car horn blasted in one long, loud honk, followed by squealing tires, a huge crash, and the crunching of metal.

Emily blinked. "That doesn't sound good."

CHAPTER THIRTY

Everyone inside the laundromat heard the crash, too, and they were too curious to ignore it. They filtered out of the Soapy Days, Tina included. "You guys heard that, right?" she asked, shooting the sisters a wide-eyed glance.

"Yeah, what happened?" Nickie asked.

"No clue."

The Hadstrom sisters were the last to step through the door. The sidewalks flooded with people now as everyone who'd heard the noise stopped to check it out.

Emily pointed, though she didn't have to. "Did that semi just hit three cars *and* the building?"

"Looks like it. That's a bar on the corner, isn't it?"

"Yeah." Nickie frowned. "I hope everyone's okay."

"Chuck's car is silver, right?" Emily asked.

"Yeah. I thought the same thing. He's not in one of those cars."

"Good." Laura took a deep breath and tightened her grip around the dagger in her hand. "We might be able to—"

The drums rose again, much closer and much louder.

Nickie winced and ducked her head. "Well, everyone's out of the laundromat. Should we do this?"

"Yeah. Come on." Laura nodded toward Soapy Days, and her sisters followed.

"We need to make this quick." Nickie stepped inside as Laura held the door open for her. "This is getting as bad as the last one. Probably worse, since that thing's so damn near."

"Okay. Just…sit on the stage." Laura helped her toward the low step.

"Here." Emily jumped up on stage to grab Nickie's Strat and hand it to her. "Play your heart out, sis. We'll take care of the rest."

Nickie let out a dry laugh and swallowed. "Here goes." She closed her eyes and focused on the pounding, furious drumbeat. Her fingers moved over the frets, the pick in her right hand fluidly strumming, and the chords to their Dad's lullaby fell into the rhythm of the drumbeat. The second she started humming, the drums both her sisters could also hear grew even louder.

"Yeah, I think that got its attention." Emily turned toward the wall of windows and watched red and blue flashing lights streak toward the crash; the patrol car's emergency siren wasn't even close to the volume of those drums.

"Don't stop," Laura shouted over the noise.

Nickie couldn't have stopped anyway. The headache was gone, but the drums beat fiercely in her head, over and over, pushing her to play the song made distinctly for the Gorafrex's rhythm.

More people trickled past on the sidewalk, heading toward the massive accident to gawk. Yet, one woman moved down the sidewalk in the opposite direction. She walked slowly, deliberately, and stopped to peer through the windows into the laundromat.

"That's her," Laura shouted. "That's the second host."

The woman faced the sisters square on with a nasty sneer. Blood covered the woman's cream-colored blouse, staining it almost black, some of it splashed up her neck and the underside of her chin.

"What *happened?*" Emily glanced at her sister as their dad's lullaby and Nickie's playing filled the air. "That's not *her* blood, right?"

Laura shook her head. "Can't be. The human's pretty much invincible until the Gorafrex checks out. So…that's gotta be someone else.'"

The Gorafrex-possessed woman eyed the three witches like a hungry predator watching its prey before the kill. Her eyes began to glow with opalescent light.

"It needs to switch hosts again. We need to draw it in and keep it in here long enough to catch it. Keep playing, Nickie."

Nickie, of course, didn't have to be told. She was in her own world, snared by the magic of the first Hadstrom on this ship who'd played the same song to put the Gorafrex away so many millennia ago.

The woman outside leaned close to the glass and flared her nostrils, like she was taking a big whiff of the three witches inside. The loud drumming now gave Laura and Emily headaches, too, but they held ground.

"Come on!" Emily shouted, motioning for the woman to come inside.

The woman's head whipped to the side, her attention caught by something. She ran away down the sidewalk.

"What?" Laura raced to the door and jerked it open, Emily on her heels. Nickie kept playing as the two sisters caught a fleeting glimpse of the woman disappear around the corner. They took off after her, but before they rounded the side of the building into the parking lot, a bright red flash cast two shadows against the building across the street. The drums cut off, and all they heard were sirens and their own heavy breathing.

Laura and Emily dashed around the corner and stopped, trying to catch their breath and find the Gorafrex at the same time. "Where is it?" Laura gasped. The huge parking lot behind the strip of storefronts, restaurants, and businesses was empty but for cars filling the parking spots. "It can't just disappear, right?"

"Did you see two shadows when that red light flashed?" Emily bent over and rested her hands on her thighs, taking huge breaths. "Man, I was not prepared for running tonight."

"Yeah, I saw them." Breathing a little easier, Laura took a tentative step into the parking lot. "There were two people here. Now there's no one."

"What's that?"

Laura turned to look at her sister. "What?"

"That. Right in front of you." Emily straightened and pointed to the asphalt at Laura's feet.

"Oh, no." Taking a few slow steps forward, Laura reached down to grasp what looked like an ordinary stick.

The minute her fingers wrapped around it, her silver ring and the stick flashed with a dull light. "Em, it's a wand."

"No…"

Turning, Laura lifted the wand as proof. "Whoever this was, witch or wizard, must've been drawn to the drumming—if that's what the elf meant when he told Nickie about it."

Emily grimaced and shook her head. "That thing just ignored us and ran here to grab another witch? Why?"

"I don't know." Laura sniffed at the air. "But I'm sure the Gorafrex took the owner of this wand."

"I smell it. It's definitely human magic." Emily pushed her hair away from her face. "This is worse than slipping into a few humans and waking up their peabrains, isn't it?"

"A lot worse. That thing's got one of us." They stared at each other. "Nickie…"

"Oh, crap."

The sisters raced out of the lot and down the sidewalk to the laundromat. Laura flung the door open and let out a huge breath of relief.

"Is she okay?" Emily asked, stepping inside behind her.

"Well, she's here. Nickie?"

The Strat lay on the stage beside her. Nickie sat with her legs splayed, forearms resting on her thighs, her head hanging all the way between them. "Hey…" Her head swayed a little, like she'd tried to lift it but couldn't even manage that.

Emily went to the stage and knelt in front of her sister. "You okay?"

"Just…really tired." Nickie sighed and started to tip sideways.

"Whoops." Her younger sister grabbed her shoulders and kept her upright. "Okay. Let's get you home."

"Did we get it?" Nickie groaned a little, and one of her arms slipped off her thigh.

"No. No, it…" Emily turned to look at Laura, who mouthed, 'Later'. "It… got away."

"But we wouldn't have gotten as close as we did without you." Laura knelt beside Emily. "That was excellent, by the way."

"What…"

"Okay, come on." Together, Laura and Emily helped lift Nickie from the stage and shuffled her across the laundromat.

"Is this supposed to happen?" Emily whispered.

"No clue."

They got Nickie to Laura's car and settled her into the passenger seat. "Hey, grab her gear."

"Oh." Emily nodded curtly. "Yeah, she'd kill us if we left her stuff." She darted inside, then came out with both iron daggers in hand. "Can't leave these, either."

"Yeah. Wanna stick one in the glovebox? Keep the other one with you. Just in case."

Emily tried not to open the compartment too hard against Nickie's knees, tucked one inside, then stared at the last dagger. "Better to be safe, I guess. See you at home?"

"Yep."

Emily shut the passenger door and went back into the still-empty laundromat to grab the amp, microphone, cords, and her sister's guitar.

Laura threw on the blinker and waited to pull away from the curb through a lineup of vehicles. She turned around on the street, away from the blockade in the intersection, emergency lights, and gawking pedestrians.

"At least nobody saw us." She lowered her hand to her lap and patted the wand left behind by the Gorafrex's victim. "We'll find your owner," she whispered.

She saw Tina and Emily talking outside the laundromat. Tina frowned in empathy and took the amp from Emily to help her load Nickie's gear into the Honda. Then Laura's phone rang.

"Oh, jeez." She slowed down to reach toward the floor in front of Nickie and snag her phone from her purse. "Sorry, sis. I have to answer." She accepted the call and put it on speaker. "Hey, Chuck."

"Laura, hey. I'm glad you answered. Look, Nickie asked me to go out and get her this certain kind of pain-reliever. I'm not finding it anywhere. Thought maybe you could help me out?"

"Um, I'm actually driving her home right now."

"What? Is she okay?"

"I think so. She uh…" Laura looked at Nickie, whose head lolled. She wasn't listening. Laura bit her lip, then lied. "She puked."

"On stage?"

"Oh, no. No. In the bathroom, right after you left. Then there was this huge car crash just on the corner, and that pretty much took everyone's attention. Kind of perfect timing, honestly. I mean, unfortunate and all, but, well, you know." She frowned and glanced again at Nickie, whose head rested against the window. A tiny snore escaped her. "She said she just wanted to go lie down. Sorry. I should've called you."

"No, that's okay. Can I…can I do anything? Bring over some soup or something?"

"We got it. Thanks, Chuck."

"Yeah, sure." He paused. "Can I talk to her?"

"Oh, um…" Laura pulled the phone away from her and faked a few dry heaves. "Probably not right now."

"Ugh. Sounds bad. Man, that sucks. Tell her to call me when she feels better, okay?"

"I will. Thanks for being awesome."

He laughed through the phone. "Uh, you too."

Laura dropped her phone into her purse and gripped the steering wheel with a sigh. "I get why you just don't think too far into the future in relationships," she told her snoozing sister, who kept snoring. "That's a lot of work, covering up with non-magical excuses." She reached out to rub her sister's shoulder. "I hope you can handle it."

Once again, Emily pulled up in her Honda only a minute after Laura had parked her Taurus outside their house. "This might be the first time I approve of you driving so fast," Laura said as they helped Nickie up the porch steps toward the front door.

Emily laughed. "Thanks? Watch this step." Nickie stumbled a little inside the front door, and her sisters stopped to look up at the discouraging number of stairs at the end of the foyer. "Just go with the couch tonight?"

"Yeah, that's probably safer." They half carried Nickie into the living room and lowered her onto the couch. Emily grabbed one of their throw blankets from the back of an armchair and covered her sister with it. Nickie moaned a little and curled up into the back of the couch. "Think that's enough?"

Emily raised an eyebrow. "Honestly, I think she'd sleep naked down here without any blankets and wouldn't notice the difference."

Laura frowned. "Yeah, we're not gonna do that."

"Nope."

Speed trotted around the corner from the mudroom, his short tongue dangling from his mouth. "Hey, buddy." Emily knelt to give him a pat hello, and he sat to enjoy the attention. Then she stood and eyed Nickie. "You think you can watch—" The bulldog sprang with uncharacteristic agility up onto the couch, spun around in a few quick circles, and curled up behind Nickie's legs.

"Speed…" Laura laughed in surprise. "Did you know he could do that?"

Emily folded her arms and shot the bulldog a playful frown. "Not even a little. He makes me pick him up every night and put him on my bed. You've been playing me, dog." Speed snorted in response and closed his eyes. "Yeah, you'll do for a guard dog, I guess."

The sisters stepped out of the living room to let Nickie and Speed sleep. They spent the next ten minutes lugging all of Nickie's gear into the house from Emily's car. Laura grabbed the wand belonging to the kidnapped witch or wizard, and they set all of it just off the foyer in the small living room.

"You brought that dagger home, right?" Laura asked, pulling out a chair to sit at the dining-room table for maybe the third time since they'd bought it.

"Yeah, it's still in my car."

"Mine too. Good place to keep it for now, I think."

"And we still have weapons at home." Emily sat and gestured with exaggerated flare toward the long iron lance and the two spheres on the table. "You think the Gorafrex didn't step inside to face us 'cause we didn't have *all* the weapons? Like, if your ring helped you make them, they're probably important."

"Yeah, maybe." Laura eyed the abandoned wand in front of her. "I think it was about to come inside, but it got distracted by whoever owns that wand. It's kinda weird that every time we get close, something comes up at the last second to help that thing get away."

"I mean, there are a lot of witches and wizards in Austin. Even more humans." Emily snorted. "It's not really that weird that people keep showing up when we're trying to recapture the most dangerous creature on this ship. Probably."

"I know. It's just frustrating. But you bring up a good point."

"Oh, I did, huh?"

"Don't let it go to your head." Laura smiled. "But I honestly don't know if we would've been able to stop that thing with just two daggers and Nickie stuck in her musical-wormhole thing. I can't shake the feeling we're still missing a piece of the puzzle here."

"Yeah." Emily drummed her fingers on the table. "Just gotta keep trying though. We'll figure it out."

"We have to. We need to find whoever owns that wand and get them away from that Gorafrex. Get them their wand back too."

The dining room fell silent a few seconds, then Emily

patted the table and stood. "I'm gonna go to bed. I'm not as tired as the witch who literally played 'til she dropped." She nodded toward the living room. "But I'm super tired."

"Long day at work?"

Emily laughed. "You could say that."

"What happened?"

"Um…you could say I practiced my stronger ring-magic in the kitchen. And it totally backfired."

"Didn't go well?"

"I mean, I got everything squared away eventually. Just had to swallow my pride first." She snorted. "Literally."

CHAPTER THIRTY-ONE

The next morning over breakfast, Laura and Emily sat down with a refreshed Nickie to explain everything their sister had missed the night before, including the wand on their dining room table and the kidnapped witch or wizard who owned it.

Pulling up in front of Hopkins' Antiques, Laura thought over that conversation and frowned. "Yeah, I think I'd be just as upset if I'd missed all that too. Now we know what mistakes *not* to make."

The bell tied to the front door jingled when she stepped inside. Carl looked up from the glowing chalice he was studying on the counter and blinked in surprise. "Laura."

"Good morning, Carl." She strode to the counter. "Good to see you too."

"Sorry." He shook his head and chuckled. "I just didn't expect to see you. Thought you'd be busy...you know. Locking *it* back up."

"Yeah, me too. Turns out we only have part of the answer. Which is why I'm here again so soon."

"Sure." Carl folded his hands on the counter and nodded. "What can I help you with?"

"First, just because…" Laura took out her phone and pulled up the picture she'd taken of the two iron spheres sitting on her dining-room table. "You ever seen one of these before?"

He squinted. "Nope."

"That's okay. Figured it was a long shot, anyway."

"What are they?"

"Some kind of weapon. I think. It's a long story." She dropped her phone back into her purse. "I'm pretty sure you can help me with this, though." Reaching into her back pocket, she pulled out the abandoned wand and set it on the counter.

Carl raised his eyebrows and smirked. "Well, yes, I've definitely seen one of these before."

"It's not mine."

"Oh."

"I need to find the person this belongs to."

He sniffed and nodded, then reached out for a long sip of already-cold tea in the chipped teacup. "That I'm quite familiar with. Just a sec." The man turned and looked over the long shelf behind him overflowing with random objects.

How does he keep track of where everything is?

"Ah." Carl held back a tower of dull, rusted crowns with one hand while pulling another item out from beneath them. He reached into a separate pile of things, rummaged around, and withdrew a second piece. He turned toward her and set down a heavy metal bowl and a wooden mallet, the round end wrapped in purple wool. "This'll do it."

"What's this?"

"*This* is a Tibetan singing bowl. Observe." Carl picked up the mallet and drew its head around and around the lip of the bowl until a low, warbling pitch rose from the counter.

"Isn't that used for meditation or something?"

"Traditionally, yes. This one, though, was crafted by an incredibly talented Buddhist monk in the mid-1700s who also happened to be a wizard. The...ringing of this bowl attaches itself to different magical frequencies, depending on anything to which its focus is directed. Such as...may I?" He gestured toward the wand.

Laura nodded. "Please."

"Excellent." Carl picked up the wand and gingerly set it inside the bowl.

Laura pointed and let out a surprised chuckle. "Did it just shrink that wand to fit inside?"

"Like I said. Incredibly talented." Carl drew the mallet around and around the lip of the bowl, and when the tone rose from the metal, the wand lit up with a red light. A faint streak of that same red glow flashed out of the bowl and shot toward the door to his shop. Laura watched it travel a little farther before it disappeared. The minute Carl stopped moving the mallet, the red glow around the wand faded. "That would be the magical frequencies. It's the best thing I've found for tracking them short of complicated spells I just don't have time to work on. And it's color-coded."

Laura laughed. "Really?"

"Yep. Red for anything over ten miles away, I believe. Orange for five to ten miles. Yellow for one to five miles.

White, of course, is less than a mile, and when it starts flashing? Well, that's when you know you're close." He reached into the bowl and removed the wand, which elongated to its normal size. Then he set it on the counter and nodded.

"Carl, you just sold me another artifact." Laura reached into her purse and smiled at him. "What's this one gonna cost me?"

"Is it part of helping you find the"—he glanced around his empty shop and whispered, "Gorafrex?"

"Yes. And you don't have to whisper. It's not the boogeyman, Carl."

He shrugged. "Might as well be, coming after wand-users." He rapped his knuckles on the counter. "Since this will help keep us all out of danger, I won't charge full price. I still have to charge you something."

"I'd be worried if you didn't."

His mouth went to the side and he tapped the counter with a finger as he appraised the situation. "Two hundred."

Laura's eyes widened, but she shook her head and opened her wallet. "I appreciate you knocking it down for me." She handed him her card. "They're always worth it when I get 'em from you."

"That's why I'm here." Carl grinned and moved down the counter to run her card.

Once she'd finished explaining how the bowl worked, Laura sat back and spread her arms. "You guys wanna come with me to find the owner of this wand?"

"Duh." Emily bit into what was left of her apple with a loud crunch.

Nickie stared at the magical singing bowl in the center of their kitchen table and folded her arms. "You know, I haven't heard the drums in over twelve hours. You think we're gonna find the Gorafrex when we find who that belongs to?"

"Maybe. Maybe not. But since you played yourself to exhaustion trying to draw the thing to us last night, we should probably wait a while 'til we try again." Laura nodded at the bowl on the table. "Right now, this is the only way for us to find out where it's hiding. And we need to help whoever it snatched up last night."

"So how does this thing work?" Nickie asked.

"Just like this." Laura set the wand into the bowl, smirking when her sisters leaned forward to watch it shrink. She moved the mallet around until the sound rose from the metal and the wand glowed orange. A red streak shot across their kitchen and went right through the dining room wall and the front of the house. "Still over ten miles away."

"That doesn't really narrow it down," Emily said.

"Right. But the direction that light just went is like a big arrow. Let's follow it."

They piled into Emily's car—not without Laura switching over the extra daggers from her glovebox—and Nickie took the backseat. "So, you just keep spinning that thing in circles, and we've got a magical GPS?" Emily glanced at the bowl and frowned.

"I guess so. Shall we?"

Emily shrugged and waited for the next flashing red streak from the bowl to tell them which way to go. She pulled a U-turn on Pressler Street, and they were off.

The bowl's magical-frequency signal took them across the river and through South Austin. By the time they passed the Roy Kizer Golf Course, the streaks of light had gone through orange and into yellow.

Emily tightened her grip on the steering wheel. "I think I'm gonna start screaming if I have to keep listening to that sound."

Nickie chuckled in the back seat. "Try drums in your head for hours, then talk to me."

Laura peered out the side window. "It has to be consistent, Em. Would you rather drive in the wrong direction and have to backtrack because I wasn't doing this often enough?"

Emily sighed. "No. I just think my eardrums are getting singing-bowled out of place. Sympathies, Nick."

"We're less than five miles. So just a little longer."

They followed the flashing and disappearing lights another few miles and turned left on Panadero Drive away from the Onion Creek Metro Park. Nickie whistled and gazed out the window. "Nice area."

Laura gazed at the large two-story homes and manicured lawns. "You know anybody who can afford living in South Austin?"

"Not well enough to have been to their house."

"Okay, where am I going?" Emily asked.

"Right." Laura ran the mallet around the singing bowl one more time, and a bright white light pointed ahead of them. "Hey. Looks like we're in the one-mile zone."

"That makes me so happy."

They slowed to follow the lights every thirty seconds or so and finally pulled up in front of a gorgeous house with two large trees in the front yard, and the light streaked past Laura's face and toward the house. The wand inside the bowl could have been a strobe light in a club, and she stopped making the bowl sing.

"This is it." Laura removed the wand, and set the bowl and mallet on the floor of the car between her feet. "Whoever this belongs to is inside that house."

"All right." Emily turned off the car and unbuckled her seatbelt. "Daggers?"

"Yeah." Laura grabbed them one by one from Emily's glovebox and handed them out. "And if the Gorafrex's inside, we just have to *keep* it inside until it has to find a new host. Then we can grab it without hurting anyone."

"Okay, let's go."

The sisters stepped out of Emily's car daggers in hand, magically concealed from human eyes despite the nice, quiet, calm, empty neighborhood. Everything about the house looked meticulously maintained and put-together... except for the shattered purple front door and the huge splinters of wood spilled into the entryway.

"That looks like it took some power," Nickie said, peering over Laura's shoulder.

"Just be careful and keep your eyes open."

"I'm not gonna *close* them—"

"Em, this is serious."

"I know. Sorry."

Laura stepped across the fractured remains of the front door, cringing when her shoe sent a large piece of debris skittering across the hardwood. Her sisters followed her into the clean, quiet home, the AC on full blast. Nothing looked out of place until they stepped into the living room.

Emily swallowed loudly.

"Oh, my god."

CHAPTER THIRTY-TWO

Two bodies sprawled across the living room rug. A shattered table and a broken armchair were toppled in the far corner, as if they'd been tossed aside to make room for the display. One was a young woman none of them recognized. A pool of blood soaked into the rug in a halo around her head, staining her blonde hair. The woman's eyes were wide open and unseeing. They couldn't make out the second body until they'd stepped farther into the room.

"That's her," Emily said, bending over to look at the woman with brown hair spilling across her face. "That's the second host."

"Oh, man." Nickie ran a hand through her hair. "Then this is the witch?"

"A dead witch. And a human who's just about to wake up in more ways than one."

"Guys?" Emily pointed toward the fireplace on the far wall. "What's that?"

Laura and Nickie stepped toward the ball of fur in the

empty fireplace, which was also matted with blood. "Jeez. Is that… a cat?"

"Why would the Gorafrex kill a cat?" Nickie grimaced.

"Probably for that." Laura stepped back and nodded at the nasty mural painted on the soft-yellow wall—a huge circle cross-sectioned into four pieces, with twelve smaller circles drawn around the outside. One of them, where the number one would be on a clock, was filled in with a pearly, opalescent substance that looked a lot like the Gorafrex's glowing light when it was about to change hosts. The rest of the diagram had been painted on the wall in blood.

"What the heck is that?" Emily stepped away from the human on the floor for a better look.

"My guess is either some kind of rune for performing Gorafrex magic…or a message. Nickie, do you have your phone?"

"Yeah. On it." Nickie pulled her phone from her back pocket and took a picture. "Did that thing leave this here for us?"

"I don't know." Laura shook her head. "But I bet if we can figure out what it means, we'll have a much better idea of what it did with that witch and what it's planning to do with others."

A low moan came from behind them, and the sisters spun around.

The brown-haired woman on the floor took a deep breath, then pushed herself up and blinked around. When her gaze landed on the blonde witch dead on her rug, she scrambled backward.

"Hey..." Emily extended a hand. "Bet you're wondering what happened here, huh?"

"I-is she..." The woman looked like she was about to hurl. Then she seemed to notice three strangers standing in front of the blood drawn on her wall. "Who are you? What are you doing in my house? Is that blood?"

"We know you have a lot of questions," Laura said. "We can't really answer them for you—"

"Your...your *eyes*. Why are your eyes silver?"

"Yep. Another awakened peabrain," Emily muttered, and shook her head.

"Oh, my god. I can't believe this. I don't—what? What am I..." The woman glanced at her hands, just like the last host once the Gorafrex left him. "This..."

"Like I said. We can't answer all your questions. You'll have to figure those out yourself. But we *can* help get your house cleaned up."

"We can?" Emily asked.

Laura raised an eyebrow at her. "Do you want regular humans all over this place, trying to solve a magical case without even knowing magic exists?"

"Good point."

"Will somebody please tell me what's going on?" the woman screamed, then she started hyperventilating.

"Okay." Nickie swallowed hard and stepped toward her, reaching out to help the woman to her feet. "We're gonna go into another room, just so you don't have to look at this. I'll stay with you until everything's taken care of. Right now, I just wanna know if anything hurts. Any scrapes or cuts or anything that you don't remember getting?"

"Uh, no. I feel fine. I just—oh, my god. Is that my *cat*?"

Nickie balled her hands into a fist and made herself carefully open them back up again. Laura leaned toward her, the color drained from her face and whispered, "She doesn't know what she did. Careful."

Nickie pressed her lips together, taking a beat. "Unfortunately, yes. But trust me, we'll get the person who did this." She turned to her sisters and shot them an exaggerated grimace as she led the witch out of the room toward the other end of the house. "Son of a bitch," she muttered.

Laura waited until they were out of earshot. "You have *your* phone on you?"

"You need more pictures?"

"No, I left mine in the car. But I'm gonna make a phone call to see who can help this poor woman clean up her house."

"Yeah. Here." Emily handed over her phone and gave herself some time to gaze at the carnage they'd stepped into. "This is awful."

"I know." Laura had called Carl Hopkins so many times, she knew his number by heart.

"Hopkins Antiques."

"Hi, Carl. It's Laura."

"Oh, hi. Didn't recognize the number. How'd the singing bowl work for you?"

She sighed. "Exactly the way it was supposed to. Now I need to find someone who can come help us…well, clean up before anyone else gets wind of this whole magical mess."

"Oh. I gotcha. Yeah, I know a few people. You wanna text me the address, and I'll send someone your way?"

"That would be great, Carl. Thank you."

"Sure. Any luck finding what you were looking for?"

Laura pursed her lips. "Not quite yet."

"Well, I know you'll stop by if you need me."

"Yep. Thanks again."

Before she could hand Emily's phone back, their dad called.

"I don't think I can talk to him and keep it together right now," Emily said. "You can answer if you want."

Laura glanced at her sister's phone. "I should." She hit Accept. "Hey, Dad. It's Laura."

"Oh. Laura? I thought I called Emily. Hey, kiddo. How's it goin'?"

"Oh, this is Emily's phone, and, well, things have been better."

"Aw. I'm sorry. Are you with your sisters now?"

"Yep."

"Good. I can ask you all at the same time. We still on for going down to the Greenbelt today so I can show you that... well, the place we talked about? I'm just out to lunch, but I figure if you girls are free, we can meet down there at—"

"Yeah, Dad, maybe we should meet somewhere else."

There was a long pause on the other end of the call. "Why's that?"

"We need to have another conversation about the family legacy." Laura glanced at Emily, who widened her eyes and nodded. "There are a couple things you don't know."

The story continues. The trio of sisters now have a second problem to solve in addition to tracking down the ancient creature hunting witches and wizards to steal their magic. It's now trying to power an ancient ship that could destroy not just Austin, but everything. Can the sisters master their magic to destroy the energy cores of the ship before the Gorafrex fires it up? Find out in *Making Magic* .

Join the Facebook Group today and find out about contests and giveaways.

Get sneak peeks, exclusive giveaways, behind the scenes content, and more.
PLUS you'll be notified of special **one day only fan pricing** on new releases.

Sign up today to get free stories.

CLICK HERE

or visit: https://marthacarr.com/read-free-stories/

Welcome to a new series in The Terranavis Universe – from the fevered minds that brought you Oriceran – that's me and Michael. We kicked it off with the origin story, The Adventures of Maggie Parker, and here we go again with **The Witches of Pressler Street**! That felt like it should be accompanied by fireworks, but I'll settle for making it bold. I started the universe earlier this year all by myself and... found out I don't like doing things on my own. I'd rather be part of a team and in particular, the LMBPN team, which frankly by now feels more like family.

In July 2017 my first collaboration with Michael came out – The Leira Chronicles – and a seismic shift in my world began. An authentic-hold-on-and-enjoy-every-minute-of-it-joyride.

Here we are again. The Magic Legacy is another beginning of another shift that came with even more growth – some of it very painful – to reveal a new version of myself. Stronger, more resilient with a few older beliefs left by the wayside and a lot of optimism for what's to come. A stronger kind of joy with a smoother ride.

Okay, a little more background is needed on how I got from here to there – where *there* is and what it all means.

Overall, I'm going to look back on 2019 as the year of finding joy again by learning how to change my mind. Real joy that permeates everything and isn't based on anything in particular going on in a day. The last year was a wild ride with the books taking off like a rocket, buying a dream house and then my oldest sister, a surgeon, died suddenly. She left behind a lot of devoted patients and a pile of debt that is getting sorted out. I mention that last part for a reason, hang on a little.

I thought over all I was fine with everything. Life gives you big events and sometimes they pile on top of each other. We keep going.

Add on top of that, I finally let go of the day job in March of this year and built a team of some great people to help me with all the moving parts of writing and publishing as an indie. All of that hit moments before I found out how much in taxes I hadn't paid yet. The seismic growth of 2018 came with a hefty bill. I was about to get a lesson in how to really run a small business.

Actually, I was about to get the opportunity to learn a few deep lessons. That is, if I was willing to sit with anxiety, confusion and pain – and not let go of all the joy that was mixed in with everything else.

Learning more about my sister left me wondering how afraid she may have been in the last year of her life, and even though we talked, there was grief and anger that I couldn't fix it, that she didn't tell us. This was paired with the knowledge that was her life to choose and her journey.

Another corner deep inside was also examining this one thought over and over again - if I was capable of creating the same financial mayhem. My brain knew I was overidentifying with her, but it wasn't stopping my heart from wondering.

Plus, looking back now I can see I was exhausted – spiritually, physically and mentally. I needed to take a break and see that I can take breaks.

Normally, I'm a fixer. If there's a problem I go hunting for the solutions. But this time, I could sense that there wasn't going to be a quick fix and just the search for one could make this longer, more protracted and more painful. Instead, I reached out to some trusted friends and started talking. I walked through every day doing what needed to be done and gave myself a break on doing it perfectly or hurriedly. It felt like I was trusting the universe to send the answers to me.

I found the right sources to talk to – financial planners about the business (not creating mayhem – did need some clarity), solid friends about the grief – even therapists. I even got some friends to join me in a book study of Brene Brown's book, The Gifts of Imperfection. The list goes on – I took someone's advice to go back to swimming and got up from my computer and went to hang out with my neighbors more. I have now seen an entire season of Bachelors in Paradise.

And all along I went on, putting one foot in front of the other and waited for answers to come to me. Truth is, there haven't been bold moments of revelation. It's been more like a gradual ease replaced by a sense of relief and trust. I'll take it. Kind of a perfect moment to step out into the world with an expanding universe and a new series with a bunch of old friends, don't you think? More adventures to follow.

First, thank you SO much for reading our stories! We can't do what we do without engaged fans

Today, I want to introduce you to another person 'behind the scenes' here at LMBPN Publishing.

If you have read anything by Martha Carr (or Judith Berens) for many months, some of our website content or wondered how we get some of our books out – you have to consider if Grace Snoke had a hand in the effort.

At first, Grace worked with Martha Carr as a virtual assistant and helped keep Martha (and all of her projects) on track. At the time, Grace was very busy and doing incredible work for Martha.

Then, some of Grace's time opened up and LMBPN was able to outsource some of our work to Grace as well. Now, Grace works with Martha and Steve for projects with LMBPN (she has many other clients as well).

I just like to think that maybe LMBPN is her FAVORITE™ client. (Hey, I can dream, right?!)

When you get a chance to meet Grace, you will immediately see her infectious smile and amazing personality. The fact that it disguises a person who is on top of a lot of projects amazes me to this day.

So, without further ado, I give you the questions to help bring Grace out from behind the scenes and allow her to become just a little bit better known.

Answers from Grace:

1. What turns you on?

Intelligence and not being shy about showing just how nerdy/geeky you are. I like it when someone will tell me facts about things I didn't know then talk more about them. Think this is why I'm dating who I am – I love how intelligent he is even though he doesn't think he is.

2. What turns you off?

Narcissism and undeserved ego. (What about deserved ego? I just have to ask. I personally waffle on this question myself as I think I really admire those who could show a bit of haughtiness but don't. However, I understand when someone who has been there-done that and has acquired a bit of assurance which – at times – comes off as a larger ego.)

3. Who do you most admire? Why?

My dad. He was a Marine who served in the Korean War. He earned four purple hearts and a silver star for his actions during the war. He went on to become a teacher and eventually a principal. He was a stubborn but loyal man, quick to anger but also quick to laugh. I miss him and the advice he gave over the years.

4. What profession other than your own would you like to attempt?
Counselor

5. What profession would you not like to do?
Teacher and/or accountant. I don't have enough patience to be a teacher and while I handle my own accounting for my business, I'm not math savvy enough to do it for others and complicated figures frustrate me. (Says the person who Martha Carr loves (partially) because she helps keep all the numbers on track.)

6. If heaven exists, what would you like to hear God say when you arrive at the pearly gates?
You were right. I understand why you believe what you believe and I do not judge you for that. I judge you on the person you were.

7. What is your favorite movie?
Hands down – The Princess Bride

"Inconceivable!"
"You keep using that word. I do not think it means what you think it means."
— **William Goldman, _The Princess Bride_**

"We'll never survive!"
"Nonsense. You're only saying that because no one ever has."

— *William Goldman, <u>The Princess Bride</u>*

"Who are you?"
  "No one of consequence."
  "I must know."
  "Get used to disappointment."
  — *William Goldman, <u>The Princess Bride</u>*

8. Who is your favorite character and from what book by which author?

Oh, this is a hard question to answer. I'd have to say Jamie Fraser from the Outlander series by Diana Gabaldon. While I don't always like his actions in the novels, they are very much in character for him as well as for men in the time period.

9. What is something most people do not know about you?

I wrote and produced a play when I was junior high school through my music teacher. Raised funds to have it done in a local playhouse with her other students.

10. What do you look forward to most in the new year?

Finishing some novels so I can quit hearing "You need to finish a novel" from my boyfriend. Admittedly, I'll probably hear "You need to finish the next novel" from him just as frequently, but that's okay. He's not wrong.

(GO BOYFRIEND, GO!)

11. What's your favorite non-LMBPN series you've done? What's your favorite series inside LMBPN?

Currently I only have one series out and that's the Little Book of Wishes series with my illustrator. I don't have any series with LMBPN... yet.

12. Do you have a web site you'd like to promote?

www.gracesnoke.com *Go check it out! Mike.*

p.s.:

"No more rhymes now I mean it!"

"Anybody want a peanut?"

"AAHH!"

— **William Goldman, *The Princess Bride***

Ad Aeternitatem,

Michael Anderle

OTHER BOOKS BY MARTHA CARR

Other series in the Terranavis Universe:

The Adventures of Maggie Parker
The Adventures of Finnegan Dragonbender

If you enjoyed this series, you may enjoy these series in the Oriceran Universe:

THE LEIRA CHRONICLES
I FEAR NO EVIL
REWRITING JUSTICE
SCHOOL OF NECESSARY MAGIC
SCHOOL OF NECESSARY MAGIC: RAINE CAMPBELL
ALISON BROWNSTONE
THE DANIEL CODEX SERIES
FEDERAL AGENTS OF MAGIC
SCIONS OF MAGIC
THE UNBELIEVABLE MR. BROWNSTONE
THE KACY CHRONICLES

MIDWEST MAGIC CHRONICLES
SOUL STONE MAGE
THE FAIRHAVEN CHRONICLES

OTHER BOOKS BY JUDITH BERENS

OTHER BOOKS BY MARTHA CARR

OTHER BOOKS BY MICHAEL ANDERLE

JOIN THE TERRANAVIS UNIVERSE FAN GROUP ON FACEBOOK!

JOIN THE PEABRAIN SOCIETY GROUP ON FACEBOOK!

CONNECT WITH THE AUTHORS

Martha Carr Social

Website:
http://www.marthacarr.com

Facebook:
https://www.facebook.com/groups/MarthaCarrFans/

https://www.facebook.com/terranavisuniverse/

Michael Anderle Social

Michael Anderle Social
Website:
http://www.lmbpn.com

Email List:
http://lmbpn.com/email/

Facebook
https://www.facebook.com/TheKurtherianGambitBooks/